Also by Harry Bryant

Hidden Palms
Snake Road

HIDDEN PALMS

Harry Bryant

ROTA Books

This is R005, and it has an ISBN of 978-1-63023-101-9.

Library of Congress Control Number: 2017936784

This book was printed in the United States of America, and it is published by ROTA Books, an imprint of Resurrection House (Sumner, WA).

Flow like water across stones . . .

Book Design by Mark Teppo
Copy Edit by Shannon Page

First trade paperback ROTA Books edition: June 2017.

www.rotabooks.com

This one is for
Elmore Leonard
John D. MacDonald
Robert B. Parker

HIDDEN PALMS

CHAPTER 1

"What do you think of the view?" Matesson asked.

I was supposed to look at the waves rolling in, at the infinite distance to the horizon, and the fluffy white clouds towering up into the sky, but closer in, there was a blonde in the pool, wearing a tiny bikini. She was slumped on an inflatable dolphin; her head was back, and her eyes were covered by big sunglasses. Her hair trailed in the pool. The bikini top struggled to contain her, like trying to wrap your hand around an over-inflated balloon.

"Expansive," I offered. "You can see just about everything."

"Some days, when the wind comes in from the west, it's even more spectacular."

I glanced down at the inflatable dolphin again, and gave some thought to what would happen when the wind did come in.

"I appreciate you asking me to drop by," I said. "But it wasn't to see the view. Spectacular as it is."

Matthew Matesson let loose with a loud bray of laughter. In the pool, the blonde jerked slightly at the sudden noise, and there was a precarious moment where she might fall off the dolphin. She wiggled her hips a few times, finding a safe spot on the slick surface. I preferred watching her instead of Matesson anyway.

He had gotten fat in the last decade. His hair had thinned out too, and the greasy ponytail hanging down between his shoulders looked like something a cat might barf up. He wore a chain of gold links that hung farther down his chest than anyone needed to know, with a matching bracelet of the same around his right wrist. His swim trunks were a size too small and a season out of date, but that had always been Matesson's style. *Never be the first*, he had been fond of saying, *but always be the last*.

1

Word was he was out of the adult film business these days. Producing indie films now. I suspected porn had paid for part—if not all—of this view, and I wasn't quite sure how the blonde fit in with earnest stories of heartbreak and emotional growth, but then, I had always been hired help. No one paid for my opinion. Then, or now.

His laugh subsided into a loose chuckle that made his shoulders quiver. "Man," he said, looking down at the blonde, "those hips—"

"Why am I here?" I asked, interrupting his train of thought. I didn't need more details. My imagination worked fine. It didn't need any help from him.

"Why are any of us here?" he asked, and he laughed again at my expression. When I turned to go, he reached for my elbow. "Hang on, Bliss. Don't be such an uptight ass."

Before I could say anything, the large glass door behind us slid open, and a blonde woman came out. She was a twin to the woman in the pool, though she wore a red bikini instead of a blue one. She was carrying a tall glass of murky liquid in either hand. "Here you go, Matty," she said, offering him one of the glasses. It had a straw wide enough for a small-caliber bullet.

"Thanks, doll," he said. He nodded at me. "And thanks for bringing one out for Bliss, too."

Her smooth and pretty face scrunched up for a second as she looked at me. "Bliss, huh," she said, and she made it sound like both a question and an expression of exasperation.

"Yep," I said. Making it sound like both an answer and an apology.

Without breaking eye contact, she lifted the glass in her hand and wrapped her lips around the straw. She sucked, dimpling her cheeks, and the level of goop in the glass dropped a finger's width. She released her hold with a loud pop—a sound I hadn't heard in awhile, not in any context like this one, for sure—and offered me the glass. She flashed Matesson a less-than-friendly glare, and then spun on her heel and marched back into the house. We both watched her go. The glass was cold in my hand, and I considered holding it against my forehead to cool me off.

"It's got ginkgo and spirulina and other shit in it," Matesson said. He sucked heavily on his straw. "Supposed to make you live forever. I don't know about that, but I do know that you're going to have the best shit of your life in about three hours."

I eyed the glass, not quite sure if I needed such an experience.

"It also puts extra lead in your pencil, for when you've got some creative work to do. Know what I mean?"

I took a cautious sip from the straw. The stuff was cold and tasted better than it smelled, which wasn't saying much. I coughed when a familiar burn hit the back of my throat.

"That's your body telling you that you need to drink this stuff more often," Matesson said.

"Is that what's going on?" I said. I took a healthier sip, and it went down easier this time.

"I figured you'd be all into this New Age healthy greens shit," he said, waving a hand in my direction.

The backhanded compliment was the best you could hope for from Matesson. Of course, I was in better shape than he was—always had been, in fact. That's what the talent does. Though, it wasn't that high of a bar to cross.

Besides, LA was a town quick to judge. No one took you seriously unless you looked like you spent most of your day in the gym.

"I stay away from refined sugar," I said. "And I get regular exercise."

"That's all?"

"That's all."

"Not doing any . . . ?"

I let the question hang there for a minute. *Any what, Matty? Porn? Drugs? Both?*

"Doing porn in prison isn't the same thing as performing for some direct-to-video compilation," I said, figuring I'd pretend he wasn't talking about drugs.

"No?" He sucked at his drink. "Too bad. I bet there's a market for that stuff. We could get there first. Totally own the space."

"You didn't ask me to come up here to talk about doing a Prison Gangbang series."

"You always have to think about the opportunities, Bliss," he said. "You never know when you're going to hit gold. You always have to keep an open mind."

I looked down at the blonde in the pool, and tried to leave my mind open, which was pretty easy when I was looking at her. "I'm going to finish this drink, and then I'm going to go," I said. I lifted the straw out of the glass, and held it over the edge of the balcony. Green goop dropped from the end and spattered on the white stone running around the edge of the pool. I let go of the straw, and watched it bounce on the stone.

I put my back to the balcony, and chugged half of the remaining contents of my glass. My throat burned, and my eyes watered, but I swallowed all the ginkgo and other shit. "You'd better start talking," I said, showing Matesson how much was left.

Matesson held up a hand. "Okay, okay. Jesus, Bliss. Don't be such a hardass."

I thought about the possible responses to that statement, and figured I should just keep my mouth shut instead. I gulped another mouthful of the green drink, and waited for him to say something interesting.

"Okay, okay," he said again. "Look. I have a little problem. One that requires a bit of delicate handling. Know what I mean?"

I shook my head.

He blew out his cheeks, and looked out over the pool. Like he was actually staring at the ocean and not the stacked blonde in the pool. "Word is you're a guy who can help a guy. You know. A little side work. For cash. No questions asked. That sort of thing."

"You want me to kill someone for you?"

"Fuck! No. Jesus Christ, Bliss. Nothing like that."

"Good," I said. "Because that's really expensive."

He blinked at me, and actually got a little pale. He sucked on his drink for a minute. "Seriously . . . ?" he started, and then stopped. As if he was embarrassed to have been caught asking.

"Let's not go there," I said. Even though there was no *there* to go.

"Yeah, yeah, okay." He nodded vigorously. "Yeah, that's not what I . . . I just—Jesus, man, really?"

I gulped a quarter of the remaining drink in my glass. "Prison changes a man," I said, keeping a deadpan expression on my face. "Makes him think about what's really important. Life. Death. All that shit. Makes him wonder what he's capable of."

"Goddamn," Matesson whispered.

Jerking his chain would have been more entertaining if he hadn't been one of the assholes who had pushed me to make one of the dumber decisions during my young, dumb, and full of—well, *those* days. I didn't blame him directly. That would be failing to take responsibility for my own actions, and it's important for a self-made man to acknowledge the choices that make him who he is. But still,

Matesson had been part of a chorus that had convinced a young and gullible mind to do some stupid shit. Messing with him now—thirteen years on—wasn't payback. That would be petty, and who has time for that shit?

Which made me ask myself why I had even bothered coming up to his house. I had put all that behind me already—shortly after I got out.

I finished the drink and put the glass on the edge of the balcony. "Thanks for the cleansing tonic," I said. "I'll be sure to thank you again in a couple of hours."

"Hang on, Bliss." He started to reach for my arm, and then caught himself. "It's not like that. It's not. Really."

"What isn't?"

"Look, I have a problem. I need someone who can take care of these sorts of things. Discreetly, you know?"

"I'm not sure I do."

"I need you to find someone for me."

"Who?"

"A friend."

"What sort of friend?" I nodded toward the pool. "Like her?"

"Nah." He inclined his head. "Well . . . you remember Gloria Gusto?"

It took me a minute to put a face to the name. "Yeah," I said. "I do."

Gloryhole Gloria. Nicknames were a double-edged sword. They made you recognizable in a field that was constantly crowded with new faces, but they also became the only way you could be remembered. Some managed to rise above the names they got saddled with. Some owned them for all they were worth, knowing such celebrity was fleeting. Bobby had been like that. Once he had claimed his name, he had lived like a king for as long as he'd been able.

I hadn't been one of the smart ones, and it took a couple of years of incarceration before that really sank in.

Two things prison offered in abundance: time to think, and time to read. I had taken advantage of both.

"She could act, and she had a healthy set of lungs. Not surprising, really. Given the rack she had." Matesson nodded at some memory, a smile greasing his lips.

5

"She came with me," he continued. "When I got that deal with Showtime. It was late-night stuff. Low budget. Rubber suits. Knockoff effects burned in during post. But viewers knew she was going to lose her shirt. And man, not only could she scream like a banshee, but she had this way of wiggling her tits when she let loose. Suits loved it. Had me shooting a picture a month for them. We could have ridden that gravy train for years. But . . ."

He shook his head.

I remembered Gloria. The studio had rented this big house up in the Canyon for a month, and had been shooting there nonstop to save money. There were always at least two crews working in the house. I couldn't recall the name of the film I had been working on that day. Nor the plot. Not that either of those mattered. Who knew what the film would be called by the time it hit the shelves? Anyway, the AD from the other film begged me to come fill a hole. They needed a fifth. I had been tired. Strung out. And I hadn't been at my best.

But Gloria? She was kind and patient and a tireless performer. She made me look a lot better than I deserved that day.

"But what?" I asked Matesson.

"Breast cancer," he said. He grimaced, and sucked heavily at his drink. "They caught it early, but it wasn't the same after that. Not because"—he gestured at his chest—"nothing like that. She just didn't . . . Anyway, the gravy train ran out of gravy. Cable took off, and they wanted smut without anyone taking their clothes off. They wanted viewers to think about people fucking, but they wouldn't hire any of us because we had reputations for actually showing people fucking, and that wasn't what they could show on cable. Dirk got a series— shot a pilot and a few episodes—and then the suits got feedback from focus groups, and word was that the viewers felt ripped off. Those who knew Dirk from Pearlescent were expecting tits and asses, and all they got was push-up bras and lacy panties."

"Uh-huh," I said. The drink was starting to make itself felt in the base of my skull, and not for either of the reasons that Matesson had mentioned earlier. I wondered about the ratio of the ingredients in my glass. My mouth tingled, and I considered leaving Matesson on the balcony—he would probably continue his bitch session just fine without me—and asking the other blonde if she could make me another one of those drinks. *I have got to know your recipe. What's the ratio of rum to spirulina?*

6

"Anyway, Gloria's been kidnapped," Matesson said, snapping my attention back to him.

"Kidnapped," I said, somewhat thickly.

"Well, not exactly," he said.

"How inexact are we talking about here?" I asked.

"It's this place. Up north," he said. "Some kind of retreat center."

"An asylum?"

He shook his head. "Not like that. It's some sort of spiritual retreat. But the guy running it is some kind of guru. He encourages his devotees to remain close during their studies."

"But they can leave any time they want to, right?"

"Sure, but they don't want to."

"Ah," I said. "How long?"

"Eight, nine months now, I think."

"And staying at this retreat isn't free, is it?"

Matesson wandered up to the edge of the balcony. He looked down, drumming his fingers on the rail. "I'm not sure it's the best thing for her," he said. "These sorts of crackpots prey on the desperate and lonely. They offer hope. A promise of a better life than what you've got. Freedom from pain and hurt and all that shit. You know what I mean?"

"Sounds like something I heard once upon a time," I said.

His fingers stopped moving. "We were all young and gullible once upon a time," he said.

"And look at us now," I said.

He turned his head and squinted at me. "Go check on her for me, would you?" he asked. "She's at some place called the Hidden Palms Spiritual Center. Up north, somewhere in the San Rafael Mountains. Not far from some speck of a town called Sisquoc. Off the 101, near Santa Maria. Go, and make sure she's okay."

"And if she's not okay?"

His face tightened. "Bring her home."

"Home?"

"Back to LA," he said. "Where she belongs. Not up there, in the woods. With that quack."

"This guy's a duck?"

"You know what I mean."

I digested his request for a moment. "You going to cover my expenses?" I asked.

"Of course."

"What about incidentals?"

"You going to type up an invoice?"

"No."

"Then I'll take your word for it," he said.

I considered that. "I'll need some to start."

His face continued to screw in on itself, making him ugly, and then something inside him unwound, and his features relaxed. "Barbara will get you what you need," he said, nodding toward the house. "Just take care of this for me, would you?" He hesitated, waiting to see if I would say anything, and when I didn't, he pressed on. "You owe me, remember?"

I nodded. I had been wondering if that was going to come up, and now that it had, well, I guess I was going to take the job.

"I'll go talk with her," I said. I nodded toward the pool and the sea and the sky. "Thanks for letting me take a peek at the view," I said.

He tried for a smile, but failed to get it arranged properly on his face.

I left him there, brooding on the balcony above the pool with the blonde and the inflatable dolphin. I was struck by the idea that he hadn't liked recalling the debt between us any more than I had, which made me wonder what I was going to find up north. In the woods. With the quack.

Barbara was in the kitchen, watching a cooking show on a small television. I put the empty glass on the counter, and she looked up from the tiny screen.

"Not quite enough rum," I said.

She smiled at me, the tip of her tongue caught in the corner of her mouth. "There might be some left in the bottle," she said.

"Matesson said you were going to give me some cash," I said.

"And . . . ?"

"I suppose we could check the bottle after that."

Her smile widened, and she crooked a finger at me to follow her.

CHAPTER 2

She was "Barbara" to my "Robert," and she got the order of things mixed up a bit. We found the bottle of rum, and there were a couple of fingers left. We shared it back and forth for a minute, staring into each other's eyes and thinking about different things. I was thinking about what I should pack in my bag for a couple days on the road, and if I should shower before taking the drive. She was thinking about what it would take to get me to put my hands on her hips.

She came up with a plan finally, and lured me into the study where she stretched out on one of the yellow leather couches. The room had floor-to-ceiling windows that looked out over the impressive view, two yellow leather couches that were soft and warm to the touch, a ceiling-mounted projector meant for watching movies on the 4:3 screen mounted on the wall, and a wall of bookcases that were filled with videos. VHS. Laserdisc. DVD.

Babs put her hands over her head and squirmed slightly on the couch, making enough noise to remind me she was there. I watched her for a few moments, rum bottle in hand, and then I wandered over to the bookcases.

"It's quite the collection," I said.

"Uh-huh," she said.

"He make all of these movies?" I asked, even though I knew the answer.

"Just the ones over there," she said.

"Over where?"

She knew I had to look at her, and when I did, she took the finger that had been playing with her lower lip and languidly pointed it to the bookcase closest to the screen. Her other hand was playing with the top of her bikini bottom.

"Right there?" I nodded. Not at the bookcase, but at the lower hand.

"Uh-huh," she said again. The other hand started back toward her mouth, but got distracted by the rounded slope of her breasts. The bikini top was really struggling to keep all of her covered.

"I might have to charge Matty extra for keeping me here this afternoon," I said. "When I should be working for him."

"Oh . . . ?"

"Hazard pay," I explained as I returned my attention to the bookcases and wandered farther away from the squirming woman on the couch.

She let out a noise that was part sigh, part throaty growl, and I almost turned around to check if she was choking on an air bubble or something. I could do the Heimlich, if necessary, and I could manage a chest massage too, especially if that wasn't medically necessary. She would probably prefer the latter to the former, which would lead to other hands-on applications.

I sighed, too. Mostly because I recognized a number of the titles on the VHS tapes. I plucked one of them off the shelf. *Lordship and Bondage 3*. Still wrapped in plastic. I looked at the cast on the back of the case, and spotted a younger version of myself. Shirtless. That ridiculous hairdo and mustache. A brunette wearing a silk nightie that didn't quite cover her ass had her hands on my chest, but not so you couldn't see her breasts, straining against the fabric of the nightie. We both looked like we were half-asleep instead of going in for a passionate kiss.

Ah, the good old days.

"That's vintage stuff," Babs said. "Matty says it'll be worth something someday."

"Does he?" I put the tape back. "Well, we'll just have to be patient then, won't we?"

She pouted. "I'm not very good at patience."

I wandered back to the couch and sat down. She immediately threw one of her legs across my lap and scooted closer to me. "I can see that," I said.

I could also see her nipples.

I took one final swig from the near-empty rum bottle and then carefully put it next to my leg, between her legs. "Matty said to get money from you," I said. "I have work to do for him."

10

"Now?" she asked. She pouted. She was pretty good at it.

"Yeah."

Her leg tightened across my lap. "But I'm not ready for you to go. And besides, you've been drinking."

"This is LA," I said. "Everyone's been drinking. And besides, the drive is all downhill from here."

She started to sit up, pulling herself closer to me, but then someone dropped several bundles of bills on her smooth stomach. A female hand snatched the rum bottle away from between her legs, and nearly brained me with it.

"Matty wants a report from you in three days." Babs' twin glared at her sister for a moment and then stomped off, swinging her hips.

I gently extricated myself from Babs' leg. "Looks like I have to go to work," I said. I started to gather the money bundles from the couch.

Babs grabbed one stack of twenties and held it tight.

"One kiss?"

"Okay," I said. "One kiss."

"With tongue."

I plucked the last bundle from her hands. "You must do all his negotiating."

Babs smiled, and when she realized my hands were full, she grabbed me by the shirt and yanked me close.

I got caught in mid-afternoon traffic coming back from Malibu, and the boardwalk along the beach was starting to fill up with the post-work crowd by the time I got off the freeway. My little bungalow was tucked back behind a mid-century rambler which was part of a neighborhood caught in a transitional phase. The throaty growl of the Mustang's engines reverberated between the houses as I slid the car up the driveway and around to the back, and when I shut off the car, I could hear the urgent bark of Mrs. Chow's Pekingese.

The dog didn't like my car. It was the sort of small dog who suffered from being a small dog in a big world, though why it fixated on my car as the source of all its canine frustration, I could never figure out.

Dogs. They make us look smart.

I collected the money-filled duffel and got out of the car.

Mrs. Chow was standing on the back porch of the rambler, smoking a cigarette. Baby Baby—always terrified, always letting everyone know—crouched behind her, growling and letting go with the occasional yip.

I nodded and smiled. Offered some small talk about the weather, which was always the same here—a half-mile from the beach in Venice. She made a face and waved a hand at the sky. I tried not to give her an excuse to regale me with the latest manner in which the sky was trying to poison her. We had enough time during our bi-weekly excursions to her favorite seafood market in Long Beach for her to catch me up on every ache and imaginary pain vexing her.

Of course, the real root cause of all her imagined afflictions was loneliness. The salons ran themselves. Her husband had taken care of the other businesses before he had been incarcerated, and now, her sons were in charge. Her daughter was finishing up a law degree at UCLA, which meant no one saw much of her. And I didn't talk much about how I kept myself busy. That left Mrs. Chow with an empty house and a high-strung dog as her constant companion— two things that are no comfort for a widow.

The California Department of Corrections and Rehabilitation had mitigated the remainder of Mr. Chow's sentence when he had been diagnosed with colon cancer. The paperwork took awhile, but he had managed to spend the last few months at home, instead of in a cell at the Colony. CMC.

We had met at Tehachapi. CCI.

CDCR was all about the acronyms.

Chow had been doing ten to twenty for money laundering, wire fraud, and tax evasion. I was doing five for possession and intent to distribute, which turned into ten by the time it was all said and done. We were innocent of all the crimes stapled to our sheets, of course, but the State of California was happy to assume there were other crimes it hadn't listed. Chow was an old man on the outs with his friends from across the Pacific, and I was a dumbass kid who had been popped for drugs. We found reasons to trust each other, and figured out a mutually beneficial relationship.

Six months after I got out, he got transferred to the Colony. A year later, he was at home, waiting for the cancer to take him. After he was gone, his son told me that the old man had wanted me to have the bungalow out back. Rent-free, as long as Mrs. Chow owned the rambler, and she was the very definition of stubborn. They were going to need a earthmover to dig her out of the house after she died.

The first night I had stayed at the bungalow, Mrs. Chow had come out and knocked on the door. She was like a fragile bird, a long-limbed heron with her pale neck and wide eyes. She had stood in the doorway of the bungalow, peering inside. "Mr. Chow says you took care of him," she had said.

I hadn't disagreed.

"He says I should take care of you," she had said.

"I'm a grown man," I had protested.

"All grown, huh? Maybe you should take care of me too?" She had laughed at the expression on my face. "No guns. No drugs," she had said.

"No guns. No drugs," I had repeated. That was easy to promise.

"You can take me shopping once in a while," she had said.

"I can do that."

"Keep your hands off my daughter, or I'll have them cut off."

I had nodded. Happy to oblige.

But then I hadn't met Angel yet.

As I walked away from the car, Baby Baby came bounding off the back porch of the house. The small dog reached the midway point in the yard, and lowered himself against the grass. He growled and snapped at the steel leviathan in the driveway, as if his earnest ferocity could somehow frighten my car and make it run away.

I keyed the alarm on the car, which made it beep once, and the noise sent the dog into a barking frenzy. I glanced back at Mrs. Chow and shrugged. What else could you do about a small dog with an inferiority complex?

She exhaled a long plume of cigarette smoke—in that way that only passive-aggressive older women can.

Hey, maybe the dog would bark himself into a heart attack. A man can dream, can't he?

I went into the bungalow and shut the door behind me, and the frenzied sounds from the yard became a distant chirrup of noise. The place was tiny; the square footage wasn't much more than the movie room at Matesson's, and it was divided up into a central living space and kitchen, a tiny bathroom, and an equally tiny bedroom. I kicked off my shoes, dropped the duffel on the couch, and was at the refrigerator in three more steps. Modern efficiency living.

Mrs. Chow opened the door before I managed three sips from the beer I pulled out of the fridge. She was prone to walking in without knocking—social etiquette gleaned from some network comedy. I locked the door at night, when there was no reason for her to be wandering around the yard, but otherwise, I didn't bother. It was like Tehachapi in that sense: during daylight, you had no privacy; at night, you were locked in—for your own protection.

Baby Baby darted in with Mrs. Chow, and bounced up onto the couch. He barked at the duffel bag once, and then grabbed the corner with his teeth and started wrestling with it.

I opened the refrigerator for Mrs. Chow, and she made a noise with her lips as she examined the sad state of affairs inside. "Nothing but beer," she said.

"And condiments," I pointed out.

"You need more leafy greens. And vegetables."

"I ate them all yesterday," I said. "And I haven't had a chance to go to the store today."

She took one of the beers, and held it out for me to twist the top off. Her hands were too delicate. Not made for opening bottles or jars. Or handling tools.

She had been a hand model, once upon a time. For one of the major national chains. She still wore a lot of jewelry, but most of it was gaudy stuff picked up on the cheap from estate sales in the valley.

"This is not very good beer," she said after taking a tiny sip.

"I wasn't planning on entertaining this afternoon," I said.

"You shouldn't cheat yourself," she said, waving the mouth of the bottle at me.

I didn't see any reason to argue with that point.

On the couch, Baby Baby was still wrestling with the duffel. He had managed to pull it closer to the edge of the cushion.

"Making movies again?" Mrs. Chow asked.

The bag had the logo of Matesson's production company on it. She knew it wasn't my bag. For all her hypochondria, very little escaped her notice.

"No," I said. "Just doing someone a favor."

"How much of a favor?" she asked.

When I didn't say anything, she looked me in the eye and sniffed loudly. "He can smell it," she said, nodding toward the fussing dog.

"Smell what?"

"What's in the bag."

"What *is* in the bag?"

She gave me a look. "How much?" she asked.

I took a long pull from my beer before answering. "It's just a favor," I said.

"How much?" she asked again.

I shrugged. "Ask the dog."

"Baby Baby doesn't know how to count. He's a dog."

"And yet, him being able to smell money doesn't seem like a stretch."

She gave me *that* stare.

"It's just a favor," I reiterated. "I'll be gone for a few days. That's all. It's nothing."

"Where are you going?"

"North. Not far."

"Into the mountains?"

"Maybe."

"There are mountain lions. You should be careful."

"There aren't any mountain lions."

"There are. I heard about one on Channel 7 this morning. Out in Pasadena. It's eaten four dogs already." She glanced over at the dog on the couch. "My Baby Baby could be next."

"We're an hour and a half from Pasadena. Like, what? Fifty miles? No mountain lion is going to come all the way here—especially through downtown and Central—to eat your dog."

"You can't be sure of that." Her rings clicked against the bottle in her hand. "You can't be sure of anything."

I kept myself from rolling my eyes. I knew where this was going.

"I'm going to pack," I said, pushing away from the kitchen counter and heading for the bedroom.

The drive up north wasn't going to take more than an hour or two, but I figured I should throw an overnight bag together, just in case this favor for Matesson turned into more than a drive up and back. He hadn't told me anything of substance about why Gloria was at the retreat, and the five grand I had gotten from the twins wasn't the sort of money thrown around for retrieving an errant child. Well, for Matesson, maybe it was. But the fact that he had called me—had called in an old debt that wasn't actually a debt owed—said he wanted someone he knew and trusted to step and fetch for him. The fact that I knew Gloria—and her background—suggested he wanted to keep the whole thing hush-hush and private.

I had lots of questions, and I was sure that a reconnoiter of the retreat was going to raise a whole bunch more. I wanted to be better informed before I saw Matesson again.

I heard Mrs. Chow's voice from the other room. "Baby Baby! Bad dog! Naughty dog!"

With a sigh, I wandered back to the main room. Mrs. Chow had gathered up Baby Baby in her arms, and she was halfway out the front door. "Must run," she called over her shoulder when she spotted me. "So much to do. Can't stay. Have a good trip." She waved and hurried out, shutting the door quickly behind her.

The dog hadn't made a noise during their exodus.

Her beer bottle, barely touched, sat on the counter next to the sink. The duffel bag was still on the couch, though it looked like it had been opened. Curious, I wandered closer to the bag, and I smelled what the dog had done before I laid eyes on the wet bills.

The little bastard had peed on my money.

CHAPTER 3

I GOT A LATER START THAN I WANTED.

After dumping the duffel bag in the sink, and running water over the stacks of bills, I had laid them out on towels and tried to use a hair dryer, but I was going to be there all night, hand-drying each bill. I settled for running them through the dryer—perma press, lowest heat setting possible—which took an hour, but at least they were dry.

I wrapped bricks of five hundred dollars in paper towels and sprayed them with some cheap cologne I kept in the bottom drawer in the bathroom. It wasn't going to entirely mask the faint, but persistence, whiff of dog urine, but it would hide the stink well enough. I dumped the bricks in a plastic sack, and put it in the trunk of my car. The duffel bag, which reeked of dog piss, went into Mrs. Chow's trash can.

And finally, at a quarter past seven, I started up the Mustang and backed it noisily out of the driveway, and headed for PCH.

I kept the windows rolled down, letting the warm air off the ocean flow through the car. The sun burned as it set, sending streamers of pink and orange fire scuttling across the pale sky. There was a storm coming, and the wind whipped waves along the shore. The air smelt of salt and sand, and for awhile, I forgot about punting Baby Baby across the lawn the next time he came out and barked at my car.

State Route 1, also known as the Pacific Coast Highway, is the scenic route up the coast from Los Angeles to all points north. The 101 is faster, but it's also miles of concrete through miles of city. Driving along the PCH lets you watch the sunset out across the Pacific Ocean. You can pretend you're not driving out of a desert basin not meant to support millions of people hustling and cursing and fucking and trying their damnedest to claw higher on their respective social ladders. You can look at all the million-dollar houses perched along the verge of the coast and daydream that one of them might be yours someday.

If the right producer noticed you and gave you that starring role in the next big studio blockbuster, that house over there with the steel shutters and the red roof could be your private hideaway from the paparazzi. If some forward-thinking record exec heard your demo, and gave you that multi-album deal, the balcony on that house that looked like a bunch of giant toilet paper tubes wrapped with Christmas lights might be where you could be puking champagne and pills on the night your first single hits the number-one spot on the Billboard charts.

I passed the turn for Matesson's house, and noticed that the view—even from the road—was impressive.

I wasn't prone to melancholic reflection on what might have been had things gone differently twenty-odd years ago. I had done enough of that during the first few years at Tehachapi, and after Mr. Chow had gotten my head screwed the right way round, I hadn't felt much urge to play the 'What if?' game. It didn't matter; what *had* happened had permanently altered whatever future that dumb kid might have had in porn. For some, Butch Bliss was just a dumb alliteration-loving motherfucker with a promising pecker, who got popped and probably pounded a few times in prison.

If I had cut a demo record after I had come out, I probably would have been one of those idiots puking off the balcony of his Malibu home. The narrative was perfect for VH-1. Popped and pounded. Maybe that could even be the title of the *Behind the Scenes* episode.

Somewhere near Oxnard, I finally had that fabled bowel movement Matesson had assured me I would be the lucky recipient of. The rum Babs had put in the drink she had originally planned for herself softened the experience. So to speak. If I had wiped my ass with one of the twenties Matesson had given me, it would have perfectly summed up the day.

I only thought about that a half-hour later. By then, it was too late.

But it was the sort of re-jiggering of events that would play well for the discerning cable crowd, in the event of a made-for-TV special.

It's important to keep track of these things. Just in case.

It was late by the time PCH turned north, heading away from the coast. I followed it through a series of small communities that weren't much more than a couple of blocks of ramshackle houses thrown up around a four-way stop. Somewhere up ahead, I knew the terrain got a little steeper, but there wasn't much to see at night. I rolled into Los Alamos around eleven, and figured that was about as far as I should bother.

A bored clerk in a generic hotel off the highway gave me a key in exchange for forty bucks, and waved a hand at the sign informing of checkout time. His duties done, he went back to his chair and put his feet up on the desk. He picked up the tattered paperback he had been reading when I had come in and got right back to work.

"Anyplace to get something to eat?" I asked. "Maybe a drink?"

He shrugged.

"How about some smack?"

He shrugged again.

"Fresh pussy?"

He looked up from his book. "You only paid for single occupancy," he said. "I'll have to charge you twenty bucks more if you have a guest."

I peeled a couple of twenties off my money clip and put them on the counter.

He stared at the money. "Please don't have an orgy in your room," he pleaded. "The owner will fire me."

"Where's the fun in Los Alamos?" I asked.

"There isn't any fun in this shithole," he grumbled.

"So where *do* you go for fun?"

He tossed the book on the desk, and gave me his full attention. "There ain't nothing out here but oil fields, quarries, and wineries, pal."

"Isn't there a prison out here somewhere?"

He snorted. "Lompoc. And an Air Force base, too. We got everything."

"Sounds like it."

I tapped my fingers on the counter for a few moments, and when he didn't say anything, I went to scoop up the money on the counter. "All right, then," I said.

"Wait, wait," he said. He dropped his feet on the floor, and levered himself out of the chair. "There's a place out on Bell Street. Near the highway interchange at Cat Canyon. Called The Rose. It's a biker bar."

"Now that sounds like fun," I said. I left one of the twenties on the bar.

"It's not a private club," he called after me as I reached the lobby door. "But, you know, it might as well be."

I nodded, and pushed open the door and wandered out into the night.

Fortunately, the hotel was on Bell Street too, and so I followed it for a few miles until I spotted the raised lights surrounding the highway interchange. The Rose was a squat single-story building on the right-hand side of the road. There were a trio of small windows along the front side of the building, but they were covered with heavy curtains. A single neon light burned in one window, advertising an American beer. The parking lot was lit by two heavy lamps mounted on the edge of the building, and there was a lot of chrome in the lot.

There was no one on the road, and so I slowed down to get a better look at the place. A trio of bearded men in dark leather vests were smoking cigarettes near the front door, and they peered at my car, presenting all manner of 'fuck off' vibe. I kept on rolling, and spotted a guy leaning against his bike in the parking lot. A woman was on her knees in front of him, her head bobbing up and down.

I didn't stop, and continued on to the highway. I took the southbound ramp and headed back to Los Alamos. The only person having any fun at the bar looked like the guy getting the blow job out in the parking lot.

I parked the Mustang at the end of the row of hotel rooms, and carried my pair of bags into the room. It was like every other generic hotel room across the country: bed, table, chair, TV, closet, toilet, bathtub. I put the bag with the cash in the closet and put my other bag on the table.

I slipped off my shoes and grabbed the remote for the TV. The bed was lumpy, and the pillows were overstuffed. There were fourteen channels on the TV, including a couple of pay-per-view options. I flicked through the late newscasts, listened to part of a monologue by one of the late-night talk show hosts, and watched fifteen minutes of some low-budget crime drama. None of it held my attention, and I finally flicked the TV off and tossed the remote aside.

I was restless. I had been doing some thinking during the drive. Matesson could have gotten my number from any number of people that we both knew, and that was primarily how I sourced work these days. Since I kept my contributions to various state and federal infrastructure nearly at zero, I had to rely on the old-school word-of-mouth referral network, which suited both me and my clients just fine. For the most part, I stayed away from the past, and it kept its distance too.

But now, here was Matthew Matesson, the guy who had directed a dozen or so of the first films I had done back in the day, asking me to track down one of the household names from that golden era of filmed adult entertainment. There was a rational explanation for why he had sought me out for this job, and most of the time, the simplest answer was, in fact, the correct one.

But there was an itch between my shoulder blades—that survival sense you developed on the inside. When you knew someone was looking at you from across the cafeteria or the yard. There was going to be trouble soon. I just couldn't figure out where it was going to come from.

Since there wasn't enough space in the room, I did some tai chi in the parking lot to unwind. And then I went to bed.

CHAPTER 4

THE COMPLEMENTARY CONTINENTAL BREAKFAST OFFERED BY THE hotel consisted of tepid coffee from a steel urn and a pre-packaged choice of either cheese or mystery fruit danish. The morning clerk was much more personable and charming than the night clerk, and I felt a little bad about not taking her up on the offer of free food.

I drove out Bell Street again, and took another look at the bar in the daylight. The lot was empty, and the building looked even more run-down in the wan morning light. Past the intersection with Cat Canyon Road was a fancy looking winery tasting room. Built in the last year or so. Its parking lot was nicely paved with clearly painted lines.

What a difference fifty yards made.

I turned onto Cat Canyon Road and drove under the highway. According to the map I had picked up while making the pit stop in Oxnard, there were two road to Sisquoc, and both took their sweet time getting to the one-shop town that was the last chance for beer and chips before heading into the San Rafael Mountains. As I drove along the winding road, up and down and around hills covered with grass and stands of chaparral, I started counting oil derricks. No wonder the road went back and forth like a staggering drunk. The only time this route had been surveyed and graded had been when the oil company had been picking spots to drop their shafts.

When I reached the eastern side of the valley, the road straightened out. On my right, the scenery became a procession of vineyards and fallow fields. By the time I reached Sisquoc, I was having second thoughts about passing on the cheap coffee and cheaper danish. The single store in Sisquoc was eclectic in its selection: everything from toilet seats to sports equipment to eighteen varieties of loose leaf tea to racks of cheap beer. Not much in the way of unprocessed breakfast foods, though, and certainly no bacon. I made do, and chatted with the old man working behind the counter for awhile. He was gregarious as all old folks in single-intersection towns are, though he wasn't too knowledgeable about *that place up the road*, as he called it.

The Hidden Palms Spiritual Center, as Matesson called it.

The old guy gave me directions. *Up the one road that runs into the National Forest*, he said. *Take the only right. If you get to Highway 166, you've gone too far.*

Easy enough.

The drive got more scenic in that 'getting out in the woods' sort of way, and eventually, I came to the singular intersection my local guide had warned me about. I took the right, and bumped along a dusty road for a few more miles until I reached a valley nestled between pine- and oak-covered hills. The road ran along one edge of the valley, and then it abruptly ended in a large gravel lot. A spur of trees swept down off the hill and sprawled across the valley floor. There was a signboard near a trailhead that wandered into the trees, and opposite the trail was a stone wall—a stirring testament to the seriousness of the 'retreat' aspect of the Hidden Palms Spiritual Center.

I parked my car next to one of the other four cars in the lot. My back was sore from all the bumps in the road, and I took a minute to stretch out my tight muscles. The sky was clearer, up in the mountains, and the air was remarkably crisp and fresh. A hawk screamed high overhead, and a light wind played with the tops of the pine trees.

Totally peaceful and picturesque. I was certain tiny rabbits would come hopping along at any moment. Little cuddly brown ones.

The hawk would ruin it, though. He'd swoop down and nab the cute one who stopped to stare at me. Predators were like that.

Thinking about the tyranny of the animal kingdom made me think about Baby Baby and mountain lions. Maybe if I started leaving bits of sirloin out . . .

The wall was more than six feet high, and it was made from red brick and concrete—locally sourced, no doubt, from one of the many quarries the night clerk at the hotel had been referring to. A metal gate covered the wide gap in the wall, where a paved road went back between rows of tall cottonwood trees. A couple hundred yards away from the gate was a white three-story house with a wrap-around porch. Beyond it, I got the sense there were a few more buildings, and looking to the left and right, I spotted well-manicured lawns and hedges. I didn't see anyone strolling about, and there wasn't any sort of guard hut near the gate.

Mounted to the wall on the right side of the gate was a plain sign that said "Hidden Palms Spiritual Center" in a nicely decorative font. Underneath the name was a notice that visitors would be seen by appointment only. Beneath the sign was a black call box. I opened it, and picked up the phone receiver inside.

A soft beeping tone sounded as I held the phone up to my ear, suggesting that somewhere a phone was ringing. As I waited, I glanced up and spotted the closed circuit camera. It was mounted on the metal brace that held the gate to the wall. I smiled and waved, trying to appear friendly.

The phone clicked, and a polite female voice answered. "Hidden Palms," she said. "How may I help you?"

"Hi, I read about this place in *Sunset Magazine*," I said. "I was in the area, and thought I'd check it out."

"I'm sorry, sir. You must have misread that article in *Sunset*—"

"Can I come in for a tour?"

"We don't do tours."

"You do appointments, though. Right?"

"Do you have one?"

"An appointment? No. Can I make one?"

The line went dead.

I hung up the phone, and took another look through the gate at the grounds of the retreat center. I still didn't see anyone, and without any other reason to keep standing there, I went back to the car to come up with Plan B.

Plan B presented itself about ten minutes later when a large panel truck rolled up the road, a fog of dust trailing behind it. A shipping company's name was stenciled on the side, and the driver brought the truck close to the gate and honked the horn three times.

I sat in my car, drumming my fingers on the steering wheel, thinking about the opportunity here. The truck was tall enough that the passenger side was hidden from the camera mounted on the left side of the gate. I hadn't seen any other cameras, but that didn't mean there weren't any, and there was only one way to find out.

The passenger door of the truck opened, and a guy in dark blue overalls jumped out. He went to the call box, and called up to the main house. He had better luck than I did, because shortly after he hung up the phone, the gate started to slide back on a track mounted to the inside of the wall.

I scrambled out of my car, and darted to the right, swinging wide of the truck. The guy in the overalls got back into the truck, and the driver started to inch the vehicle closer to the gate as the metal barrier rolled on its track. I sprinted to the wall, and as the truck rolled forward, I ran toward it. The truck bumped across the metal track, and just as its rear wheels bounced over the bar, I ducked around the corner of the open gate and dropped behind the nearest hedge.

The truck shifted gear, spewing a cloud of diesel fumes out of its exhaust, and went on up the drive between the cottonwoods. The motor driving the gate engaged, sliding the metal barrier back in place. I stayed in a crouch, breathing heavily. Waiting to see if anyone had noticed my daring effort.

Within a minute or so, the gate finished closing and the miasma of diesel fumes dissipated. Birds kept chirping. A cloud drifted in front of the sun. The trees kept photosynthesizing and the grass kept growing. Nothing else moved.

I peered around the edge of the hedge, taking a better look at the grounds of the retreat center. The hedges were well groomed, and the grass was healthy and mowed regularly. I spotted a couple of heavy benches positioned beneath older cottonwood trees, the sprawling branches of the tree making for good shade. In the distance, I spotted a couple of wooden stakes in the ground. They had colored rings painted on them, and when I spotted metal hoops rising out of the grass nearby, I realized it was a croquet setup.

And that settled the mental conversation I'd been having with myself. It looked like guests had access to the grounds. I stood up, and dusted off my jeans. I was going to stick out more if I tried to be sneaky, and so I wandered toward the main house as if I was just out for a bit of fresh air.

Off to the left of the main house was a small parking lot with a handful of expensive-looking cars. Wings extended off the main house to the left and right. The left-hand wing made a right angle, and the right wing connected to a square building that didn't have any windows. I caught sight of the panel truck behind the building, backed up to a loading dock. The road continued around the warehouse/receiving building, and it terminated in a second parking lot where there were more cars—most of them looked like the sort driven by working-class folk.

I kept strolling, walking parallel to the wall on my right, and as I passed the truck, I got a glimpse of the two guys hauling pallets of wrapped supplies into a well-organized warehouse space. There were a few oil drums lined up next to the raised loading dock, along with a pair of heavy dumpsters.

Past the warehouse, the rest of the main house came into view. The front and the extended wings were the crossbar of a 'T,' and the long leg was a single-story structure with lots of windows that terminated in a boxy add-on with thin windows that made me think of a church. Behind the house, I caught sight of sunlight reflecting off a pond, and beyond a row of stiff pine trees, there was a rounded shell, like some sort of outdoor amphitheater.

Voices drifted across the parking lot, along with an occasional splash as someone dove into the pool. A pair of women wearing gold uniforms—matching skirts and blouses—appeared from the direction of the pool party. One of them was pushing a cart, laden with linens and dishes, and the other was carrying a basket of bottles. They walked along the concrete path, and I figured they were heading for the kitchen—where the truck was unloading.

I ignored them, and continued along the outside edge of the parking lot. Beyond the lot, a dirt track continued farther back and I figured it looped around toward the amphitheater. Past the shell, the trees got thicker—somewhere back there the wall took a left turn. I spotted a couple of men, wearing uniforms of the same color as the ladies, working near the broad lawn in front of the wood and stone platform.

Keeping my pace casual, I angled toward the voices, and before long, I found myself at the edge of the pool. There were two pools, actually. One was long and narrow, and was probably meant for those industrious types who wanted to swim laps. The other one was irregularly shaped, lined with white stone. There was an artificial waterfall at one end and a diving board at the other end. A handful of small tents with drapes that could be raised and lowered at the whims of their occupants were scattered between the long pool and the meandering pool. Adjustable lounge chairs were arranged along the side closest to me, positioned so as to best capture the path of the sun as it crossed the sky overhead.

"Well, hello, there." A woman reclining on one of the deck chairs had noticed me. She was wearing a saffron-colored bikini and a floppy white hat covered her head. A tall glass, sweating heavily in the sunlight, sat on a small table next to her chair. "I don't recognize you," she continued, pulling her dark glasses down an inch to peer at me over the rims.

"I just got in," I said, throwing myself onto the chair next to her. I leaned over and held out my hand. "I'm Robert."

"Julia," she said, taking my hand. Her grip was cool and distant. Her eyes were blue, but distracted. Like she was half-listening to some concerto only she could hear. "You haven't even been to orientation yet, have you?" She giggled lightly. "They don't usually let you wander around dressed like that."

I realized everyone in the pool was wearing swim attire the same color as Julia's bikini. I stripped off my shirt. "Better?" I asked.

She made an agreeable noise as she sipped from her cold drink. Her gaze, while hidden by her sunglasses, traveled from my neck to my groin and back up again. "Better," she sighed. "Almost . . ." She sucked on her drink again, her gaze wandering back down.

"I don't have a swimsuit," I pointed out.

She raised an eyebrow and shrugged.

"Hey, Julia. Who's our new friend?" One of the guys in the pool had noticed me.

She raised a languid hand and waved it dismissively. "He's *my* friend," she called out.

"Can he come play with us?"

She looked at me again.

"I don't have a swimsuit," I reiterated.

"He's not dressed for the pool," Julia said loudly, sounding a bit put out.

There was laughter from the water, and then something landed with a wet splat on the deck near my chair.

"He can wear mine," a male voice said, and there was more laughter and playful shrieking from a couple of the women in the pool.

"You can wear his," Julia said, nodding toward the sodden lump.

"Well, when in Rome . . ." I said.

As I stood up, Julia lay back on her chair, adjusting her hat so she would have an unobstructed view of me as I took off my pants. A warm smile curled across her lips. I wasn't bothered with her attention. I had been naked in front of strangers before. But what made me pause, belt half-unbuckled, was the presence of the two men in white behind the row of lounge chairs. They hadn't been there moments before. They had broad shoulders and thick arms that strained their uniforms. Like two sausages stuffed into a single casing.

"You need to come with us," the one with the thicker eyebrows said.

"I guess I shouldn't have skipped orientation after all," I said to Julia.

She looked up at the musclebound pair. "You couldn't have waited five minutes?"

The silent one shook his head.

"They take all the fun out of things," she sighed.

I nudged the wet swimsuit with my foot. "There's a guy in the pool with no trunks on," I said, trying to be helpful.

"Charles?" She shook her head. "I've seen his penis. Plus, he's been in there for an hour. It'll be all shriveled and wrinkly."

The silent one of the pair came around the chairs and stood real close to me. "Let's go," his friend said.

I picked up my shirt. "Maybe next time," I said to Julia.

She gave me a smile that said she doubted there would be a next time, and judging by the tense scowl on the face of the dude in my personal space, she was probably right.

CHAPTER 5

WE WALKED AROUND THE OUTSIDE OF THE MAIN BUILDING, heading for the wing that crooked at a right angle. The silent one walked ahead of me, and the other guy stayed real close on my heels. They set the pace, and we didn't walk fast, but we certainly weren't out for a leisurely stroll. I looked to my right, spotting a row of small structures out behind the trees and hedges, and for my curiosity, I got slapped on the back of the head.

"Eyes forward," the talkative one said, in case I hadn't figured out what the smack was for.

I complied. Mostly to not antagonize the pair. I matched the silent guy's stride without thinking—old muscle memory from years of shuffling in lines, trying to not stick out. I kept my head still, but my gaze flicked back and forth, trying to see as much as I could without being obvious.

The row of houses looked like tiny cabins, but they were neither fancy looking nor entirely utilitarian. Rustic, without being rough hewn.

And then we reached the end of the wing, where the silent dude opened a door and glowered at me as I went past him and into the building. I paused just beyond the doorway, not sure which of the half-dozen doors off this hallway was our destination, and I got a shove in the back for that stutter step. "Over there," the talkative one said, and I just kept walking.

He'd stop me when it was time.

Our destination was the third door on the right, and I got slapped again when I overshot. I gave the talkative guy a eyeful this time, letting him know I was keeping track. He glared back at me, the muscles tight in his neck. Daring me to do something. His right hand was already clenched.

I made fish lips at him, and then danced through the open door before he could do something he'd regret later.

The room was an administrator's office. Big desk by the window. Heavy carpet on the floor. A couple of chairs on this side of the desk. A walnut bookcase along the wall to my left, filled with serious-looking books that had long multi-syllabic titles. There was a sideboard on my right, and a large oil painting was centered on the wall over the table.

Seated in the leather executive chair behind the table was a thin man in a black suit. His shirt was the color of the staff uniforms, and his tie was the color of the guest clothing. Unfortunately he was enough of a ginger that his hair and goatee clashed slightly with the color combination, which is probably why he went with the black suit. To cut down on the color matching confusion.

The desk was clear but for a phone, a large leather notebook, a crystal glass filled with an inch or so of dark liquid, and a pad of lined paper.

Undirected, I sat in the chair farthest from the door. I hadn't bothered putting my shirt on yet, and the guy behind the desk noticed my physique with a wrinkle of his nose.

"Who is he?" Desk Guy asked the two security goons.

Silent guy shrugged.

"You didn't search him?"

I started to stand up.

"Sit down," Desk Guy snapped at me.

I sat.

"Stand up," the talkative goon said.

I looked at the guy behind the desk. "Which is it?" I asked.

"Oh, for fuck's sake," he said. He waved a hand in our general direction.

I figured he was giving us permission to do the dance, so I stood back up and stepped away from the chair so that one of the two security guys could check me out. The talkative one did the deed, slapping his hands along my pockets and pants. I made a little noise as he slapped my ass, and his face reddened as he pulled my wallet out of my back pocket. "Sit down," he said, shoving me toward the chair. He put my wallet, my money clip, and the remote fob for my car on the desk.

"Thank you, Terrance," Desk Guy said.

Terrance, heretofore so talkative, merely grunted in reply. He and his pal stood near the door, looking like the musclebound apes they were.

Desk Guy scooted his chair closer to the desk, and leaned forward to grab the contents of my pockets. It was a big desk, and Terrance had put them down close to the outside edge. I thought about getting my wallet for him, but figured that would only make things more awkward than they already were, and so I sat there and watched.

Desk Guy dismissed the remote control fob quickly. Not much to it. A couple of buttons, and there were only three keys on the ring. One was obviously for the car, and he didn't care about the other two.

My wallet was almost as minimalist. Desk Guy looked at my license, and then thumbed through the cards I had: Ralph's customer card, video store punch card, library card, proof of insurance. A couple of receipts. He dropped my wallet on the desk with the same dismissiveness as the set of keys.

He wrinkled his nose slightly as he picked up the money clip. The clip itself was silver, finished with a textured pattern of fish and birds. He slid the money out of the clip, and idly thumbed through the wad. He put both down on the desk, but not back the way they had been.

"So, Mr. Bliss, I have a bit of a quandary," he said, leaning back in his chair. He steepled his fingers on his stomach. "Perhaps you can help me."

"I'd be happy to," I said.

"The Hidden Palms Spiritual Center is a private facility," he said. "Our guests come here because they want to get away from the noise and headache of . . . wherever they come from. They want to be forgotten. Anonymous. Invisible. And they pay quite readily for that service."

"I imagine they do," I said.

"My job"—he indicated the pair by the door—"*our* job is to make sure they get what they pay for. Do you follow?"

"I do. It's not that complicated."

"But you"—he leaned forward to look at my license—"Mr. Robert Bliss, of Venice, California, are not a paying guest at the Center. Nor are you employed here."

"I would agree with both those statements," I said.

He sat, staring at me. I stared back. Near the door, one of the terror twins cleared his throat. The office had air conditioning. Even without my shirt, I was happy to sit there all morning. Even with a desk as clean as his, Desk Guy looked like a busy man. I could wait him out. I had lots of practice.

There were a number of parallels between shooting porn and sitting in prison. Some more evident than others.

The pair of guards should have just escorted me off the premises. But they hadn't. They had brought me in for this sit-down. The guy behind the desk had wanted to know who I was.

The real conversation happens in the silences. I learned that in Tehachapi. No one ever shoots for subtlety in a dick flick. Not even the French at their New Wave avant-gardest.

Still, this guy could use a nudge. I was, after all, here to find Gloria.

"That lady by the pool," I said. "Julia? Was that her name? Anyway, she was real nice. She asked me to join her and her friends in the pool." I indicated the shirt in my lap. "That's why I'm not wearing my shirt. Your friends here didn't give me a chance to put it back on."

"I see," Desk Guy said.

"Should I put it on now?"

"Whatever makes you most comfortable, Mr. Bliss."

"I appreciate that, Mr.—?"

"Wilson," he said. "And it's 'Doctor' Wilson."

"Oh, my apologies." I looked at the walls again, making sure I hadn't missed the ubiquitous set of diplomas. "Doctor of what?" I asked.

"Psychology," he said. His shoulders lifted slightly. "And Philosophy."

"Really?" I lifted my shirt and slid it back over my head. "That's impressive."

He made a tiny gesture as if all the work had been a mere trifle of time and effort.

"And you're the man in charge around here?" I put my arms through the sleeves of my shirt.

"I ensure the smooth operation of the Center and the continued comfort of our guests, yes."

"That's a lot for one guy to manage," I said. I indicated the pair by the door. "What about these guys? GEDs? Or do they have advanced degrees too?"

"Mr. Bliss—"

"Me? I took a couple of classes at community college. After high school, of course. But I could never sit still long enough for all those lectures. And then, you know, *later*, the opportunities were more, shall we say? *remedial.*"

"Mr. Bliss," Wilson interrupted me. "I really don't care about your education. Or lack thereof." He leaned forward, and put his hands on the desk. "What are you doing here?"

"I was making new friends," I said.

He glanced at the pair, and nodded slightly.

Terrance stepped forward, and clouted me on the ear with one of his ham-sized fists.

"Ow. Son of a bitch." I wiggled in the chair, rubbing at my ear. The chair hopped on the carpet, changing my angle to both the desk and the door.

Terrance didn't return to the door. He stayed close. In case Mr.—sorry, *Doctor*—Wilson gave him the nod again.

"As you noted, I am a busy man," Wilson said. "I really don't have time for shenanigans. And so, I'm going to ask just one more time: what are you doing here?"

"Visiting friends," I said.

And when Wilson's eyes flicked toward Terrance, I moved first.

I pushed out of the chair, driving my right fist straight at Terrance's groin. My fist wasn't as big as his, but my knuckles were a lot harder. And he wasn't wearing a cup. He let out a whoof of air and bent over, which put him right in line with my knee. His head snapped back, and his body went stiff. Then he collapsed like a tree falling in the woods.

Silent Dude was a faster thinker than he was a talker, and he had already processed what was happening. I kicked the other chair in his path as he charged at me, and he stumbled over it. I kicked him once in the ribs to suggest he stay down, and when that didn't seem to convince him, I kicked him in the head.

I fussed with the bottom of my shirt for a second, giving everyone a moment to adjust their expectations to the changed situation.

Wilson hadn't moved from his chair. When I looked at him, he leaned back and let the chair swivel a bit from side to side.

"You're a busy man," I said. "I shouldn't keep you from whatever it is that you need to be doing."

He didn't say anything, but the hint of a smile worked at the corner of his mouth.

I gathered my belongings from the desk, and then I picked up the glass that had been sitting next to the leather notebook. I sniffed its contents. Scotch. At this time of day?

"I'll let myself out," I said, putting the glass back down on the desk. "Just out there, and to the right?"

He nodded, and watched me step carefully around the two goons who were groaning about their oncoming headaches. I had to shove Silent Dude's legs out of the way to get the door open, and Wilson called my name as I was about to leave.

"If you walk straight out of this building and go directly to the gate, I'll have someone open it for you. Otherwise . . ."

I got the hint. There were more dudes like the pair on the floor, and now they'd know I wasn't as much of a pussy cat as I let on. "Straight on through, and then out," I said. "I can manage that."

"Very well," Wilson said. He gestured toward the glass on his desk. "Not a fan of fifteen-year-old Scotch?"

"I have simpler tastes," I said.

CHAPTER 6

Back at the car, I had a conversation with myself.

"Shit. Shit. Shit shit double shit."

Not my best conversation with myself, but it hit all the highlights.

Since there wasn't much else to say in that regard, I started up the car and drove away from the Hidden Palms Spiritual Center. Drumming my hands on the steering wheel as I sped along the dusty road. Angry at myself for letting things get out of hand. Angrier still that I hadn't expected something like that to happen. Had I actually thought I could waltz in and wander around without someone noticing?

Well, I had, I guess. But the situation had gone sour awfully fast. At Tehachapi, there was more posturing, more dancing around the act of violence. Everyone talked about doing it, but you didn't, really. And if it did happen, you didn't see it coming, and it was brutal and final. Outside, people laid hands on each other without any respect for personal space. Behind bars, your space was the only thing that remained yours. You encroached on someone else with care.

Which is to say that Terrance should have seen the dick punch coming. It wasn't my fault that he wasn't wearing protection or that he was an idiot. I couldn't be blamed for those things.

But it shouldn't have gotten that far. Something felt off, and I didn't think it was entirely my fault.

I was still replaying the last few minutes in Wilson's office when I reached the main road. I glanced in both directions, checking for cars, and then let my gaze come back to center again.

The old dude at the store had said to make the first right, and he hadn't bothered to tell me that I could have also made a left off the paved road. Which wasn't a big deal at the time, because I was looking for Hidden Palms. Now, though, I was interested in the road opposite the one that led to the walled retreat center.

The road itself wasn't any different than the one I sat on now, but sitting on the shoulder were a pair of bikes. Two burly-looking dudes with leather vests, sunburned arms, and dark glasses were sitting on the bikes. Calm as you please, like they were waiting for a delivery van to trundle by with parcels or something.

I clicked on the turn signal, checked once more for other cars, and then pulled out onto the main road. I kept an eye on the pair of bikers in my rearview mirror until a curve of the road hid them from view, and I kept thinking about them all the way back down to the main road that ran across the valley.

There was no reason to go back to Sisquoc, and so I turned left at the bottom of the hill, and headed back to Los Alamos.

I drove past the Los Alamos exit with the bar and the winery tasting room. The tasting room was open, and the bar was not. I kept on, blinked as I passed through Los Alamos, and then I took the first exit on the other side of the small town. I worked my way back along the frontage road, where I learned there weren't any other hotels, and so I ended up at the same place I had stayed at last night.

The same clerk was still working the desk, and she recognized me. "Good afternoon, sir," she said cheerfully as I came into the air conditioned lobby. "Is there something more I can help you with?"

"Is there a phone I can use?" I asked. "Do you mind if I call LA?"

"Well, I will have to charge you for long-distance services," she started.

I pulled out my money clip and peeled off a twenty. "How's this?" I asked, putting it on the counter.

"That works," she chirped. "Would you like change?"

I shook my head. "Just let me know if I run over, okay?"

She nodded and pointed me toward a black phone over by the coffee urn and breakfast station.

I dialed Matesson's number, and while I waited for someone to answer, I looked over the table. The number of plastic-covered danishes looked about the same as this morning. Either she was an efficient restocker or the other guests shared the same opinion of plastic-wrapped cheese goo as I did.

A woman answered the phone, drawing my attention away from the mystery of the danishes. "Hey, it's Bliss. Is the man of the house around?"

"Hi, Butch. It's Babs."

"Hi, Babs. Is he there?"

"Oh, Matty? Gosh no. He's at the studio."

I knew what "at the studio" meant back in the old days. Was that still the case, or was there an actual lot somewhere now? It didn't really matter, did it?

"Can you give me the number over there?"

"I can, but it probably won't help you," Babs said. "It's just the main number."

"What about a cellphone?"

"He never has it on when he's working" she said. "It's so annoying." She stretched the 'o' out into something resembling a purr. I wondered if she was even aware that she was doing it, and then I realized I didn't care if she did know. I was just glad she was.

And that thought was getting away from the reason I called . . .

"So, uh, maybe you could tell him I called," I said. "He can . . . never mind. Just tell him I called."

"Okay," she said. "I'll tell him."

"Maybe I'll try again tonight."

"I don't know if that'll be a good idea," she said.

"Why not?"

"There are some people coming over to the house tonight."

"What kind of people?"

"Fun people, silly."

"Of course they are," I said. Which translated to a party. Which then translated to "don't bother calling tomorrow either." I sighed, and rubbed my left ear. The one Terrance had popped. "I'll try later this week," I said.

"Okay," she said, and before I could say anything else, the line went dead.

"Okay," I echoed, and quietly hung up the phone.

The desk clerk smiled when I returned to the counter. "That was less than three minutes," she said. "I won't charge you." She slid the twenty back across the counter.

"Keep it," I said.

She hesitated. "I'm not sure I . . ."

"Well, I could use another room, I guess," I said.

"Yes," she said, her face breaking into a smile. "I can take care of that for you." The twenty disappeared off the counter. "The same room as before, Mr. . . ."

"Bliss," I said. "And no, another room would be fine." I glanced out at the double row of rooms. "Something on the second floor, perhaps?"

"Second floor it is," she said. "And for just one night?"

"Make it two—no, three. Three nights."

"Three nights," she echoed. "I have just the room for you. On the second floor." She glanced over my shoulder. "Is that your car?"

I looked. "It is," I said.

"Mustang," she said, almost to herself as she flipped through a stack of paperwork on the counter near her computer terminal. "'78?" she asked.

"Pardon me?"

She found the piece of paper she was looking for, and I spotted my loopy signature on it. "Here we are," she said. "I have all your details from last night. I can put these in the system again."

"Oh," I said. I looked back at the car again as she started typing.

"'76," she said. "It's a 1976 model, isn't it?"

I figured out what she was talking about.

"Yes," I said. "It is."

She nodded. "I still get those two mixed up. The '78 and the '76. It's the King Cobra versus the *not* King Cobra styling. Not that yours is either. Just, you know . . ." She trailed off with a bit of a nervous laugh.

"You know something about cars," I said. Look at me, being clever.

She nodded. "Yeah, I see enough of them every day. Plus my brother works at the Shell station down the road."

"You're local," I said.

She shrugged slightly. "Mostly."

I let her type for a minute. The top of her head was level with the base of my throat, which made her somewhere around five foot six or so—depending on how sensible her shoes were. Her auburn hair was pulled back into a twist that was bunched up at the back of her head, making her face look more tense and tight than it probably was. She wasn't heavy, nor was she thin. She was somewhere in between, and probably had to eat and exercise appropriately to not fall one way or the other. She wore a silver ring on her right hand, middle finger, but nothing on her left. A silver chain with a tiny cross on it hung on the outside of her lavender blouse, and she had tiny silver hoops in her ears. She was more tan than her office job suggested, and there was some muscle definition in her upper arms. Her name tag read "Dolly," and I wondered if that was short for something else. Like "Babs."

"Okay, Mr. Bliss," she said as she finished keying everything into the computer. "Will you be paying cash again?"

"I will." I started peeling bills off my clip. "Can I just pay for all three nights now?"

Hotels got nervous with cash customers, and I didn't have a credit card, so everything went more smoothly when money changed hands up front.

"Sure, uh, absolutely, I mean," she said, eyeing the fold of bills on my clip.

"And, Dolly?" I paused for a second. "Can I call you Dolly?"

"What? Oh, yes, of course." She laughed. "That's my name, after all."

"It is," I said. I put money on the counter. "Call me Butch, please."

"Butch?"

I nodded.

"Okay, Butch. I can do that."

"That's great, Dolly." I finished counting out enough for all three nights. "Can you tell me where the locals go to eat and drink around here?"

"You mean, like not where all the tourists go?"

"That's exactly what I mean."

"We don't get that many tourists," she pointed out.

"Well, you shouldn't think of me as one, then," I said.

"I won't," she said happily. She fondled the money for a moment, and seemed to be on the verge of saying something, but then she ducked her head and fussed with the cash drawer instead.

I looked at the top of her head as she made change. My right knee twinged a bit, reminding me of what it had been doing earlier, and I wondered how much of a headache each of the Terror Twins were having.

"All right," Dolly said, and she counted out my change on the counter. And then she added a tiny folio with a couple copies of the room key to the pile. "You'll all set, Butch."

"Thank you, Dolly," I said. I scooped everything up.

"And you should check out a place called Rye."

"Rye?"

"Go that way two blocks, take a right, and it's on your left. It has a green and red front. You can't miss it."

"I won't," I said. I tapped the edge of the paper folio on the counter for a second. She stared at me, an eyebrow half-raised. I was trying to decide if she was a compulsive restocker or not.

"This place—Rye—what time does happy hour start?" I asked.

She smiled. "Four," she said.

"And what time do you usually get there?" I asked.

"Four fifteen," she said. Without hesitation.

Precise, then. But not necessarily a restocker. Good to know.

CHAPTER 7

RYE WAS A CONVERTED TWO-STORY HOUSE WITH AN ENTIRE parking lot to itself. The trim was green, and the building itself was red. Made it look sort of Christmasy, but not in a kitschy way. The windows were covered with industrial blinds, but framed with delicate curtains. There was a beer garden out back that was easily as large as the restaurant itself. There were a dozen or so cars in the lot already. I parked my car near an old cottonwood at the western edge of the lot—the sun was edging toward the top branches of the tree—and walked across the hot asphalt to the front porch of the restaurant.

Inside was dark and cool and noisy. To my left was a hallway that led to bathrooms and a closed door marked for employees only. To my right, a handful of large television screens were mounted in the corners of the main room, which was easily half of the ground floor. A long walnut bar curved along the wall opposite the windows. Behind it were floor-to-ceiling racks of booze, and the racks were broken up by large lamps that blessed that side of the room with warm, yellow light.

Beer taps were placed at either end of the bar. At the back of the room, a large pair of French doors looked out on the beer garden, and to the left of the doors was an archway that led back to a kitchen.

There were two pool tables, a dart board, and a quartet of pinball machines. Tables were scattered throughout the room in a haphazard fashion that suggested they had once been set in neat rows, but at least two rowdy weekends had passed since that time, and no one had bothered to line the tables back up. A jukebox off to my left was slowly cycling through the hits of the '80s, quietly jetting out a miasma of nostalgia from a hidden pipe in the back.

Ah, good times.

There was a stool near the front door, along with a podium, but there was no one checking IDs at the door, and so I wandered across the room and sat on a stool on the left side of the center of the bar. I was examining the plethora of American-made whiskey when a dark-haired bartender with tattoos snaking down her right arm came up and slid a coaster onto the bar in front of me.

"See anything you like?" she asked.

I made eye contact and kept it. "How often do customers think you're talking about something other than booze?" I asked.

"You'd be the first," she said. "Today," she amended when I raised my eyebrow.

"My faith in humanity remains misplaced," I said.

She shrugged. "The tips are good."

"How about the bourbon?" I asked.

She glanced over her shoulder. "Lots of choices, sport. The expensive stuff is higher up. It'll cost you if I have to get out the ladder."

"How about you grab me something from a shelf comfortably within reach and pour me a glass," I said. "Neat. Please."

She stretched for the higher shelf and poured me a generous shot. I took a small sip, and sighed as the warm bourbon coated my throat and dripped a trail of fire down my throat. "That's nice," I said.

She shrugged. "You asked nicely."

"It was a rule my mother insisted I learn."

"Just the one?"

"The only one that stuck."

"Still, I'm sure she's proud."

I took another sip, so I didn't have to respond.

She got the hint. "Food menu?" she asked, moving on to safer topics.

"Sure," I said.

She retrieved a single sheet of paper and left it on the counter next to my glass. "Happy hour starts at four," she said. "But it doesn't apply to bottles on the upper shelves," she added. "So there's no reason to pace yourself unnecessarily."

"Good to know," I said. I glanced around the room. "This place fill up much at happy hour?"

"Pretty good," she said. "You passing through this afternoon?"

"No," I said. "Here for a few days."

"Staying up on Bell Street?"

"Is there anywhere else?"

She shook her head.

"Sounds like I made the right choice then," I said. "Clerk at the hotel said I should check out this place or some bar near the highway. Called the *Ruse* . . . ?"

"*The Rose*," she said. "Yeah, out by Cat Canyon. Pretty rough place. Compared to here." She nodded toward the bottles behind her. "And definitely not the same selection."

"I'm two for two, then," I said, lifting my glass and toasting her.

She smiled as she pushed away from the back counter and leaned against the bar. "I'm Freesia," she said, offering me her hand.

"Robert," I said, offering her mine. Her grip was cool and courteous. "Nice to meet you."

"You too," she said. "I'm going to check on some other customers and then come back. You can tell me what looks good on the menu, and I'll tell you whether or not you're right."

"Ah, the pressure," I said.

She laughed as she wandered off. It sounded somewhat like her handshake, but there was a note of actual amusement in it somewhere.

Instead of examining the menu, I looked at the rest of the patrons in the room. There were only about eight of them, scattered around the room at a few tables, and they were interesting enough to keep me from the menu. As I finished my clandestine survey, a door opened at the back of the hall past the arch, and light spilled into the hall.

A guy walked in, and by the time the door shut behind him, he had disappeared to my left, presumably into the kitchen proper. I didn't think much of it at the moment, but when he came back and paused for a second at the door, listening to someone talking to him in the kitchen, I looked up from the menu. He looked familiar, and it took a second for me to remember where I had seen him. He had been in the passenger seat of the van that had pulled into Hidden Palms a couple of hours ago.

Freesia was talking with the other bartender, a beefy-looking dude with a crew cut and rolled-up sleeves on his polo shirt, and she broke off her conversation with the bartender and started walking back toward me. I busied myself with the menu, so as to not get caught flatfooted, but she wasn't coming to talk to me. She sailed right on past my spot, and greeted two men who were easing themselves into seats to my left. I heard leather creaking, and I smelled sweat and leather and oil.

"How are you guys doing this afternoon?" she asked. She followed up with "Beer?" before either of the newcomers could respond.

They both ordered the same thing, and as Freesia grabbed a couple of pint glasses and started to fill them at the nearby taps, I casually looked over.

Both of the biker dudes were staring at me.

"How you doing?" I asked, being neighborly. I raised my glass of bourbon in a polite wave.

"Good," the shorter of the pair replied. His hair was short too, but he still had the obligatory bushy beard and tattoos crawling out of the collar of his jacket. His face was sun-darkened and his squint was permanently creased into his forehead. "You?" he asked.

"Can't complain," I said.

Freesia put two full pints in front of the men, and they picked them up. The taller one drank heavily, his throat pumping beer down his gullet. The second one raised his glass to me before taking a long pull from the foamy glass.

"You need to see menus today?" Freesia asked.

"Nah," the one biker said. "We're good, doll."

Her face froze up a bit, and the line of her mouth tightened. "Four bucks each," she said.

"We might have another round," the biker said.

"Still eight bucks for this round," she said.

The taller biker nudged his companion who put his beer down long enough to dig a crumpled bill out of his jacket pocket. He tossed it on the bar. "He'll have another one," the biker said, nodding to his friend, "but I'm good for the moment."

Freesia drew another pint before she picked up the crumpled bill. The taller biker finished his first beer, burped noisily, and started on the second. The shorter guy continued to sip his beer slowly, and out of the corner of my eye, I watched him look around the room— mostly as an excuse to check me out a few more times.

I didn't respond to the attention. It was happy hour, and I was hungry.

After tossing the bikers their change, Freesia returned to check on me.

"I'll have the tacos," I said.

"Beef, chicken, or pork?" she asked.

"Pork," I said.

She took the menu and wandered off to place my order.

In the back, the door opened, spilling light into the bar, and a shape hauled a stack of boxes on a handtruck into the kitchen.

Kind of late to be delivering groceries . . . I thought.

"Bitch," the biker said.

"What's that?" I realized he was talking to me.

"Our waitress," he explained. "She's not very personable."

I turned slightly on my stool. "I noticed that," I said.

He had a bit of a smirk on his face. The patch on the shoulder of his leather jacket showed a snake wrapped around a dagger. There was blood dripping from the dagger, and it looked like the snake was squeezing the blade so tightly that it was cutting itself.

"Maybe she doesn't like new faces," he said. The smirk became a thoughtful twist of his lips.

"I was here five minutes before you two," I pointed out. "Which makes me an old friend, relatively speaking."

"But we might have been here yesterday," he countered. "While this is your first time."

I tipped my glass in his direction. "You are correct on the latter, which makes it impossible for me to argue counter to the former."

His companion finished his second beer, belched again, and got off his stool. He glared at me a second, and then stomped off toward the front door and the bathrooms. The back of his jacket had the same logo, only much larger, and along the bottom were the letters "CMFMC."

"He doesn't like you," the remaining biker said.

"Was that what he was saying?"

"You seem like a smart guy. Maybe too smart for your own good," he said.

"I've heard that before."

"Smart guy like you probably thinks he knows something about citrus farming."

45

"What sort of farming?"

"Citrus. You know, oranges, lemons."

"Yeah, I know what oranges and lemons are. I'm not sure why I should give a shit beyond that . . ."

He took a long drink from his glass, staring at me over the top of the rim the entire time. He belched as he put the glass down on the counter with a loud thunk. He slipped off his stool and came close, sizing me up, and I noticed how clean and tight his tattoos were. They weren't as faded as I would have expected on a leathered lifer. "Be smart," he said ominously.

His gaze flicked to my right. "Keep the change, doll," he said, and then with a final fiery eyeballing just for me, he walked off. His buddy was waiting by the door, and they pushed out into the afternoon sunlight.

"What an asshole," Freesia said. She had been hovering nearby, and she went to clear their glasses. Her opinion didn't stop her from pocketing the bills left on the bar.

"Pretty good tipper for an asshole," I said.

She leaned against the bar near me, as if she was sharing some intimate secret. "Money doesn't make someone any less of an asshole," she said. "It just makes them think that it's okay for them to act like that."

I thought about Matesson, and couldn't fault her line of reasoning.

"You want another one?" she asked. "That asshole is buying."

I was smart and said *yes*.

CHAPTER 8

DOLLY WAS PROMPT, AND WE PRETENDED TO NOT KNOW EACH other at first. After Freesia brought her a drink, I offered the opinion that she seemed familiar, and she laughed at my ignorance, and then I remembered where I had seen her before.

She moved over a stool, and we blew past the introductory game that people play at bars, and by the time she finished her first drink, I had learned that "Dolly" was short for "Dorothea," and she had learned that "Robert" was my real name versus "Butch."

She had added a little bit of makeup since I had seen her last, and while we were waiting for her second drink to arrive, she undid the twist in her hair and ran her hands through it several times.

I was on my third or fourth drink, which meant I was feeling liberated and loquacious.

"Wow," I said.

"What?" She tucked some of her hair behind her ear.

"That's quite the transformation," I said.

"I just let my hair down."

"And I'm glad you did."

Freesia put another daiquiri on the bar, and she refilled my water glass. "Any food?" she asked.

"Yes," Dolly said, eager to not be talking about her hair anymore. "Can I have the hummus plate?" She looked at me. "Did you want to get something?"

"I ate already," I said. "Tacos."

"Just the hummus then," Dolly said to Freesia, who nodded and wandered off before I could order another glass of bourbon. Probably on purpose.

"You haven't told me what you do for a living." Dolly pulled her drink closer. It was a strawberry daiquiri with a red straw.

Some things were consistent in every bar in the world.

I watched her lips close around the straw.

"This and that," I said.

"Are you working on *this* or *that* right now?"

"A little of both."

"Does it get confusing?" she asked. "Keeping them straight."

"Not really."

"It sounds confusing."

"You get used to it."

"Do you ever get to do *stuff*?"

"As compared to *this* and *that*?"

She nodded, closing her lips around the end of the straw again.

"Once in a while," I said. "Usually on a Thursday."

"There's a Thursday this week," she pointed out.

"Handy."

"Any *stuff* planned?"

"Depends on how *this* and *that* go."

She sighed heavily. "You are a very busy man."

She laughed, and I laughed with her. When she turned slightly on her stool, our knees bumped under the bar.

I didn't mind.

"How long have you been working at the hotel?" I asked.

"Awhile," she said with a shrug and a coquettish curl of her lips.

"And before the hotel?"

"This and that."

"I see how this is going to go."

"You started it."

"I did."

"You want to try again?"

I took a drink of water as I thought about answering her question.

"I missed most of this decade because I was in prison," I said.

"Me too," she said. "I mean, missing the decade part. I was in school."

"For what?"

She laughed. "I was going to ask the same thing. *For what?* Isn't it funny how that question works for both of us?"

"I would have rather been in school," I said.

She put her elbow on the bar and leaned her head against her hand. "I can imagine," she said, the levity gone from her face.

I connected her change in mood with something she had said earlier. "Your brother, the one who works at the Shell station, he did time, didn't he?"

She closed her eyes as she nodded slightly. She rolled her head off her hand and reached for her drink. "He was young and dumb, and now?" She shrugged. "He's older and dumber, but he's still my brother."

"Any other family?"

"Dad was in the Air Force. He dragged David and Mom and me all over the world. Vandenberg was his last post. He died of a heart attack right when we were starting high school. Mom didn't see any reason for us to move again. She thought we'd appreciate staying in one place long enough to make friends."

"Here in Los Alamos?"

She shook her head. "No, over in Santa Maria."

"So what are you doing working in Los Alamos?"

"What were you in prison for?" she asked, deflecting my question.

I thought about deflecting too, but decided to be honest with her. "Drugs," I said.

Her face changed, and her knee moved away from mine.

And that told me something else about her brother.

"How about this weather?" I asked, changing the topic. "It's been the same for what? Eighty days now?"

"Eighty-five," she said.

"What happened on the eighty-sixth day?"

She made a face. "Fog."

"Fog? Really?"

"Haven't you ever seen fog before?"

"We call it an inversion layer down in LA," I said.

She laughed. Some of her perkiness was coming back.

I had almost said *We don't get fog in prison*, but that would have been the wrong joke to make.

Her hummus arrived, and I managed to catch Freesia's eye this time for another drink. My toes were warm, and the little counter in the back of my brain reminded me that this drink should be my last one—Freesia's careful ministration of a round of water between rounds of bourbon notwithstanding—but the company was pleasant, and I was inclined to ignore that reminder.

It had been a long day, after all. Lots of driving around. Not much to show for all the work except for getting tossed out of Hidden Palms. Oh, and dick punching a security guard.

I almost deserved an extra drink for that.

"What are you thinking about?" Dolly asked.

"Oh, just someone I ran into today," I said, rousing myself from the mental replay of the afternoon.

"Someone you know?"

"Not especially."

"What are you doing in Los Alamos?" she asked.

"That's an awfully personal question," I responded.

She shrugged. "You've dodged all the other personal questions. A girl can keep trying, can't she?" She nudged the hummus plate toward me, indicating that I should have some. The plate was loaded with soft pita triangles and a whole mess of salty and savory additions to layer on.

"A girl should keep trying," I said. I took a pita triangle and some hummus to be polite. The tacos had filled me up, but when an attractive woman indicates you should share her food . . .

"So?"

"I'm looking for a friend," I said.

"Like a bounty hunter?"

"No, not like a bounty hunter? Why would you think that?"

"It's the way you said 'friend.'"

"How did I say it?"

"Like they aren't really a friend."

She raised her shoulders as she smeared hummus on a pita and then layered feta and a tiny tomato on top.

Freesia returned with my drink, asked Dolly how she liked the hummus just as Dolly shoved the loaded pita into her mouth, and then smiled as Dolly made unintelligible noises around the mouthful of food.

"She either likes it, or she's choking," I translated for Freesia.

"I've been doing this long enough to know the difference," Freesia said.

"It's nice to be in the hands of a professional," I said.

She quirked an eyebrow at me, and she smiled again when Dolly managed to swallow and actually articulate an opinion about the food.

"They do that on purpose," Dolly said after Freesia wandered off.

"What do they do?"

"Ask you if you like the food when your mouth is full."

"It's an important perk of the job," I said. "Balances out the leering jackasses and the drunks who vomit on the bathroom floor."

"God," Dolly said. "I don't envy them that. There was a guy at the hotel last week who made a real mess in the bathroom in his room. The maids complained about it for days."

"That wasn't the room you put me in, was it?"

"Oh no. It was down on the ground floor."

"I bet you see all sorts of interesting characters at the hotel."

"You have no idea." She took a sip from her drink. "But we're not talking about them."

"We're not?"

"No." She tucked her hair back behind her ear again and looked at me. "Why are you looking for your not-friend?"

"It's a favor."

"For who?"

"Another friend."

"There you go again. I don't think this person is your friend either."

"Someone I know, then."

"And the first friend? The one you're looking for? How do you know she's in this area?"

"I didn't say it was a woman."

Dolly gave me a look. "But it is, isn't it?"

"Maybe."

Dolly shook her head. "Men always get vague when they're talking about women."

I smiled at her. "Is that so?"

She returned the smile. "You're easy."

"Not *that* easy."

"No?"

She blushed lightly as soon as she said the word, and she busied herself with her hummus for a moment. I picked up my glass and took a tiny sip. The bourbon was a trickle of warmth sliding down my throat.

"She's up at the Hidden Palms Spiritual Center," I said. "I drove up there today, and tried to see her."

"Did you?"

"They wouldn't let me in. Not without an appointment."

"Did you get one?"

"An appointment?" I shook my head. "Not exactly."

"I've heard about that place," she said.

"What have you heard?"

"Rich people go there. Hollywood types. But not, like, important Hollywood types. Not the sort that you'd read about in those glossy magazines you buy at the store."

"Right. Not A-listers. More like the next tier down."

"The guy who runs it is an ordained minister. Of something— what is it?—oh, yes, the First Church of the Holy Relic."

"The what?"

"The Holy Relic."

"Which relic?"

"The holy one, I suspect."

"Well, they're all holy. You wouldn't have a Church of the Marginally Special Relic, would you?"

"Probably not a church that celebrates a crap relic either."

"I think you mean *garage sale tchotchkes.*"

"Five for a dollar?"

"Exactly."

She thought about that for a minute. "It's more of a free-wheeling religion, though," she said. "You know, every Saturday. Before ten."

"Free-wheeling, huh?"

She smiled, her teeth around the end of the straw in her drink. "You like that?"

"I see what you did there. All those housewives, driving around neighborhoods, checking out garage sales. Fighting over the boxes of relics."

"I'm right, though, aren't I?"

"I think you might be."

"I like being right," she said. She rocked on her stool a bit, her knee bouncing against mine.

I thought about the amphitheater I had seen at the retreat, mainly so I wouldn't think about her knee banging into mine. "So, this minister dude . . . what's the connection with the Spiritual Center? Do you have to join his church to stay there? Do you have to listen to sermons and take Sunday School lessons?"

"I don't know," she said. "I've just heard stories."

I waited.

"What?" she asked when the silence went on too long.

"I want to hear the stories."

"They're just rumors," she said.

"So?"

"They probably aren't true."

"You want to talk about why you're in Los Alamos instead?"

She wrinkled her nose at that question. "That wasn't very nice," she said.

"I'll make it up to you later."

"Promise?"

I gave her one of my most charming smiles. She saw something in it that made her blush again, and while she busied herself with her hummus, it was my turn to apply pressure to the contact between our knees. I felt her leg tighten and push back.

"What do you do when you're not trapped behind that desk?" I asked.

She furrowed her brow as she held a hand in front of her lips, her jaw moving around a mouthful of food.

Silly man. Asking a woman a question when she was eating.

I traced a finger down her bare arm. "This isn't the skin of a woman who sits in an office all day," I said. "She gets out into the sun. Regularly."

"Surfing," she said after she had swallowed.

"Really?"

She tightened her arm so that her muscle definition was more definite, and I saw that as an excuse to touch her again. "You ever done it?" she asked.

"Surfing?" I shook my head. "It looks like a lot of work to not get wet, and then you get wet anyway. And I bet water goes up your nose a lot."

Dolly smiled at me. "If you're any good at it, water doesn't go up your nose."

"Yeah, but how long does it take before you reach that point?"

"How long does it take for a person to get good at anything? Before you went . . . you know, before—"

"Prison?"

"Yeah, before that. What did you do before? And don't say 'this and that.'" She read the cagey glint in my eye.

53

"I was in the movie business," I said.

"Doing?"

"Movies."

She shook her head at my obstinacy. "Regardless, whatever you were doing there, it took awhile before you got any good at it, right? But that didn't stop you from trying. You wanted that job. You wanted to do good at it, and so you kept working at it. Working through those moments when water went up your nose, or whatever the equivalent was for you."

I thought about what the equivalent of *water going up your nose* would have been on a porn shoot.

"Fine," I said, shrugging off *that* mental image. "I never tried it because I was lazy and a bum. That better?"

She laughed. "You are not a bum," she said.

I inclined my head at that, but didn't say anything to contradict her. "You were going to tell me stories," I said, reminding her.

She ran her hand through her hair, and let out a long breath. "Can we not do that?" she asked.

"Do what?"

"That thing where you ask me all sorts of questions, and I answer them because I like sitting here with you, and you listen to me because while I think you like sitting here with me too, I suspect you're probably more interested in these stories than me."

"That's not true," I said.

"Okay," she said. "But let's stop right there, so I don't have to find out if you're just being polite."

"Okay," I said. I took a drink from my glass. I repositioned myself on my stool so I was turned even more in her direction. "Tell me about surfing," I said. "Convince me."

She laughed.

And she was very convincing.

At least two drinks later, we left Rye and stood awkwardly in the parking lot. The sun had vanished, leaving fading trails of gold and rose in the west, and there was a salty tang in the air. Sea change. Weather was coming.

She pointed at the grey sedan parked near the middle of the lot. "That's mine," she said. She turned and pointed over toward the tree at the edge of the lot. "That's yours."

"It is," I said. I was standing between her and the restaurant, and my line of sight covered part of the road along the restaurant. There was an SUV parked down the street with a rack of lights on its roof. It had a two-tone paint job.

"Are you okay to drive?" I asked.

She nodded, pushing back her hair from her face. "I think so. You?"

"Not quite yet, I think."

Her teeth worked her lower lip. "Maybe you should walk me to my car."

"I can do that."

She was steady as she walked. I had to concentrate a little to not sway and bump into her. Not that she would have minded, but I didn't want to give the guy in the police car any extra reason to follow me back to the hotel.

Dolly unlocked her car, and I held the door for her as she climbed in. I was a little disappointed that there hadn't been some last contact between us, but she quickly powered down the driver side window.

"I would like nothing more than to offer you a ride," she said, looking up at me. "But I'm afraid that if you get in my car, I will not drive you back to the hotel. Instead, I will take you and a towel I have in the trunk to one of my favorite spots along the beach, and we will get very naked and very sweaty."

I crouched down, and rested my arms on the door of her car. "How sweaty?" I asked.

"Very, very sweaty."

I thought about leaning into the car and kissing her, and it was clear she was thinking the same thing too. As I leaned, she touched a button and the window started to rise. I had to move my arms, and off balance, I took a step back from the car.

She stopped the window halfway up. "Good night, Bliss," she said. Her lips remained parted. Her breathing was shallow and quick.

"Good night, Dorothea," I said.

"Dream well," she said.

She started her car, and with a last, lingering glance, she drove out of the lot and turned right. Away from the parked cop car.

I stood in the parking lot, listening to the sound of her car grow fainter.

The police car didn't move.

I closed my eyes, and imagined that I was on a surfboard, rolling back and forth with the swells. I exhaled like she told me I should when I was on board, letting my breath take out all the tension in my legs and arms. Until there was nothing left of me. *That's how you have to be*, she had said. *There is no you; there's just the board and the sea.*

I opened my eyes, coming back to myself, and glanced up at the darkening sky.

It was a nice night. The hotel wasn't that far away. I might as well enjoy the walk.

I went to my car, and retrieved my bag from the trunk. A couple of cars passed on the road, and when I got to the sidewalk in front of the restaurant, the cop car was gone.

CHAPTER 9

WHEN I GOT BACK TO MY ROOM, I REALIZED I WASN'T ALONE A second before someone's fist rocketed against one of my kidneys. I dropped my bag and sagged a little. Someone grabbed the front of my shirt and hauled me fully into the room, tossing me onto the bed. The door was shut, and before I could twist around and get my bearings, I got smacked in the lower back two more times.

I slid off the bed with a groan, and lay still, my chest and face pressed against the comforter on the bed.

"Be smart," someone said, and I recognized the voice and the advice.

His voice came from over by the door, and he hadn't been the one hitting me. The hitter was the taller one, the one who drank his beer fast and hadn't liked me—as was evidenced by his keen desire to do damage to my kidneys.

"I'm working on it," I said.

The room was dark, and I should have noticed that the shades had been pulled as I had wandered along the open-air balcony in front of the second-floor rooms. I hadn't been up here yet after checking in earlier, and this place wasn't so classy that the maids would do a turn-down service at the end of the day. They left the curtains open in the rooms, and the guests closed them when they checked in. I had been thinking about other things.

And now I was wondering if I was going to be pissing blood later. So many things to think about.

I heard the zipper being pulled on the duffel, and a small flashlight clicked on. The biker let out a low whistle. "What have we here?" he asked no one in particular as he dumped the contents of my duffel out on the table near the window. He played the light across the scattered clothing, my toiletries bag, the small camera

I had packed along, and the narrow stacks of plastic-wrapped twenty-dollar bills.

"It's—" I started, but my sentence was cut short by a quick jab to the kidneys again. The left one, this time.

"Hang on, Brace," the biker said. "There's probably a very good explanation for this." His light flicked in my direction, the beam dazzling my eyes. "So let's hear it."

"Fuck you," I said. I jerked my head toward the guy behind me. "And him, too."

The light went steady, shining right into my eyes. I closed one eye and turned my head away so that I wasn't completely blinded. As it was, I was still seeing spots.

"You sure you want to go with that?" the biker asked. "After I reminded you about being smart."

"I'm not the one breaking and entering. And assaulting."

"So?" he asked, and I didn't bother answering his question. The light flicked back to the table, cataloging the contents of my bag again. The biker moved closer to the table, and just before the light clicked off, I saw his gloved hand moving toward the stacks of bills. In the darkness that filled the room after he put his light away, I heard leather creaking.

"Go home," he said when he was done putting things that didn't belong to him in his pockets. "This is your only warning."

"Who's warning me?" I asked.

"Hey, Clint, can I hit him for that?" a deep voice behind me asked.

Clint laughed. "No, Brace. Not tonight."

"Tomorrow?"

"Maybe," Clint said.

"I'm busy tomorrow," I offered. "How about the day after?"

"You won't be around the day after tomorrow," Clint reminded me.

"Maybe," I said.

My eyes were beginning to adjust to the gloom in the room. Clint was a darker blob against a not-quite-as-dark background. The tall one—Brace—was standing between me and the TV on the table next to the wall opposite.

"Go ahead," Clint said to the guy behind me.

Brace moved, and my head rocked against the comforter. He had slapped me with his meaty palm, which didn't hurt as much as getting a kidney pounding with his fists, but it wasn't a love tap, either.

In any case, my skull was better suited to getting banged around a bit than my kidneys.

I growled, giving Brace the impression that he was pissing me off, which was the reaction he wanted to hear. I heard his feet shuffle on the carpet and the leather of his jacket creaked. But before the big man could punch me again, the light clicked on.

Clint wandered over to the bed, shining the light right in my eyes. I turned my head away, and he grabbed my hair to hold me still, and brought the light up close. I pinched my eyes shut, and he twisted his hand in my hair, pulling my head back. "Go home, tough guy," he hissed. "You're not wanted here."

He released his hold, and my head flopped against the bed.

The light went out, and Clint moved away from me. "We're done," he said to the bigger man. "Leave him."

I remained still, and the door opened. They were briefly outlined against the glow from the lights in the parking lot, and Clint glanced back into the room before he closed the door. "Thanks for the donation, asshole," he said as he shut the door.

And then I was alone in the room. Slightly poorer for the inter-action, but I knew their names now, at least. That was something, right?

I put the chain on the door after they left, and leaving the lights off, I peeked out around the edge of the curtain. I didn't spot them in the parking lot for a minute, but then the lobby door swung open and the pair came out. The shorter guy was laughing, and they wandered around the edge of the building and disappeared. A few minutes later, I heard the sound of motorcycles starting up, and a pair of bikes drove past the hotel lot shortly thereafter, heading up Bell toward the highway. Toward the Rose.

I went into the bathroom where I shut the door and turned on the light. Peeling up my shirt, I inspected the damage. There were going to be bruises tomorrow, but nothing that wouldn't fade after a few days. I splashed some water on my face, and then stared at my reflection for a long moment.

Assholes will be assholes, I thought. Mr. Chow had said it like it was some sort of Zen truism. Not quite a koan, because there was no puzzle to decipher, but like one of those maxims that inextricably explained the whole universe via some esoteric subtext. It took me a few years to figure it out what he meant.

I switched off the light in the bathroom and went to turn on the light in the other room. I inspected the scattered contents of my bag, verifying that the smaller of the two assholes who had been in my room had, in fact, taken all the money I had in the bag.

Three grand.

I made a mental note to get it back before I left Los Alamos.

I wandered out of sight of the hotel, and in an empty parking lot of a chiropractor's office, I did tai chi for awhile. Cleaning my head and loosening the tightened muscles of my back and neck. The sky got darker, and the temperature dropped a bit. The smell of salt got stronger in the night air, and I saw a few bats fluttering around aimlessly before the sky darkened enough to hide them.

Mr. Chow had led a group of us every morning in the yard at Tehachapi. At first, he had been the only one who looked like he knew what he was doing, and often the Brothers had made catcalls and obscene gestures, which he steadfastly ignored.

The rest of us—and in the beginning, it had been me, Dicky, Tattoo Bob, Wang and Chung, and Lin—did our best to mirror his glacial and graceful movements. Very quickly, I had realized that the movements were only part of what Mr. Chow was doing. We were learning how to quiet our minds and passions. How to focus our energies on what was truly important and vital to our well-being.

I was learning tai chi from Mr. Chow because I owed him my life. I had pissed off a noisy black man named Lando, though I never did find out what had set him off. Not that it mattered much in those days. I was a fresh fish, and he probably just wanted a piece of me to prove something to the rest of his gang. I was in the showers—by myself, not having realized that the room had cleared out—and suddenly there was Lando, with a shiv he had made from a mattress spring and a plastic spoon.

And then Mr. Chow showed up, moving like a ghost. Lando had turned, slipped sideways, and then fallen, bleeding from a self-inflicted puncture wound in his neck. Mr. Chow had pressed a finger to his lips, and then vanished as quickly as he had appeared.

Just like that. Me, standing there naked, and a big black man, bleeding out in the prison shower. When the guards showed up, Lando was dead and I was still in shock.

Much much later, I learned that Lando had been bumping Mr. Chow in the cafeteria, trying to make the older man drop his tray. He never succeeded because Mr. Chow always saw him coming, but it had been a tiresome game.

Assholes will be assholes, Mr. Chow had said when I had confronted him.

I got extra time added to my sentence because of that, I pointed out.

No, Robert, he said. *You would have died in that shower. Instead, you got* more *life. That is a gift. What are you going to do with it?*

You're an asshole too, I said.

See? Already, you are taking advantage of this gift to become more enlightened.

Every once in a while, I still missed him.

The only cars in the parking lot at Rye were my Mustang, a pair of vehicles near the back that probably belonged to the staff, and the blue and white SUV that had been parked down the street earlier in the evening. I stopped near the edge of the lot and watched the uniformed officer shine his big flashlight into the interior of my car. The lettering on the side of the SUV identified the vehicle as belonging to the Santa Barbara County Sheriff's Office, and the inquisitive deputy was a medium-sized man with a bit of a gut and a big flat-brimmed hat.

I watched him look for excuses to mess with my car for awhile, and then I dug out my keys and tapped the alarm button on the remote two times. The alarm on the Mustang shrieked once, and then went quiet, but it was noisy enough to spook the deputy, who jumped back from the car. He swung around like he was looking for the hidden camera crew, and his wiggling light finally swung in my direction.

"Can I help you with something?" I asked as I approached. My hands were empty and visible. I had slipped my keys in my back pocket.

"Who are you?" he demanded, shining the light at my face.

The parking lot was lit by sodium lights in each corner, and while it wasn't the brightest of lots, it was bright enough that the light in the face was unnecessary, but apparently, it was my night for getting flashlight burn on my retinas.

"I'm the owner of that car," I said, raising a hand and blocking his light. "Is there a problem here?"

I should have gone around the block and come back when he wasn't poking around my car, but I was tired, and I didn't want to give him time to work up some excuse to have the car towed. Not that it would be all that good of an excuse, but once the car was off the lot and in the hands of a towing company, it would no longer be his problem. Assholes, remember? The world was full of them, and Los Alamos's share were rapidly making themselves known.

"Let me see some ID," the deputy said.

"No," I said.

"Excuse me?"

"Is there a problem?" I said again.

"There will be in a second," he said.

"Probably. Especially after you violate my Constitutional rights protecting me from unlawful search and seizure."

"Hang on. Now listen up . . ."

"Uh-huh," I said, waiting for him to get to the point. And when he didn't, I prompted him. "I'm listening . . ."

He lowered his flashlight, and flicked it toward the car. "That's your vehicle," he said.

"That's what I said."

"You've been drinking."

"Not that you can tell," I said.

"I saw you come out of that establishment there."

"Not recently, you haven't," I said. "You were too busy looking through the windows of my car to notice that I walked all the way down this block from Bell Street."

"No, I mean—"

"Oh, you mean, earlier, when you were parked across the street?" I nodded. "Right. Right. But if I came out of this bar then, what car did I get into?" I gestured at the Mustang. "Mine's still here. And I'm not in it. Kind of tough to pop me for drunk driving when I haven't even gotten in my car yet. Should I go back into Rye and count to ten and come out again? Will that be enough time for you to go hide?"

He started walking toward me, his flashlight beam playing across the pavement between us. "Okay, asshole, that's enough of that."

I waited until he got close enough and then I raised a hand to stop him. He did, and I noticed that he had made no move toward his sidearm. "What's the message?" I asked tiredly.

"What message?"

"The one you're supposed to give me," I said.

"What are you talking about?"

"You're less than ten yards from me," I pointed out. "And your gun is still secured. If I was a real threat, I could get over there, take your flashlight from you, and severely beat you with it before you could even get your gun out. Which means you're either an idiot, or you know who I am and you've got something you want to tell me. I'm going to be polite and assume you're not an idiot."

He shuffled from foot to foot for a second, and then he clicked off the beam on his flashlight. "Good night, Mr. Bliss," he said. His gaze wandered over my shoulder. "And I hope your drive back to LA tomorrow is pleasant."

"Thank you, Deputy," I said. "But I'm probably not going back to LA tomorrow."

He smiled at me, his teeth gleaming in the light of the sodium lamps. "I'm delighted to hear that," he said.

"Why am I not surprised?" I asked rhetorically.

"I'll be seeing you," he said.

"I'm sure you will."

He walked over to his car, got in, and noisily drove out of the parking lot. I remained where I was, and watched him make his dramatic departure. Only then did I turn and look toward the bar behind me.

Standing out back were a pair, smoking cigarettes. I recognized Freesia, and the dude standing next to her was an older man with a scraggly white beard, wearing a cook's apron.

I waved. They waved back. I got into my car and drove back to the hotel.

This town, was the last thought running through my head when I crawled under the covers on the lumpy bed and tried to box the pillow into a comfortable shape.

CHAPTER 10

I SLEPT IN, AND AFTER EXAMINING MY BRUISES IN THE BATHROOM mirror, I showered and put on a clean shirt. I finished putting away the few items from my bag that I wasn't going to need during the day, and then I went down to the lobby to check out the choices on the breakfast table.

"Good morning," Dolly sang out as I came into the lobby. Her hair was plaited into a single braid today, and her blouse was the color of the morning sky after a night of cleansing rain. Her lips were shiny and rosy, and they looked a lot moister than the tiny poppy seed muffins laid out in precise rows next to the coffee urn.

"Good morning," I responded.

"Do you sleep well, Mr. Bliss?" she asked.

I was about to respond when the door to the back office opened, and a gnomish man in an ill-fitting suit poked his head out. He mumbled something unintelligible to Dolly, who nodded her head, and then he stared at me for a few seconds. He had bushy eyebrows and a layer of grey hair that looked like it had been shellacked to his head. He mumbled something that was probably supposed to pass for genial office conversation, and I smiled and nodded as if I agreed wholeheartedly. He disappeared back into the office, shutting the door behind him.

"I thought gnomes turned to stone if they were exposed to sunlight," I said.

"He's not a gnome," Dolly said. "He's the night auditor."

"There's a difference?"

She smiled at me as she finished shuffling together a stack of printouts. "I slept well," she said. "Once I decided to go to sleep, that is." She gave me a knowing glance as she took the stack to the office where the gnome was hiding out.

There hadn't been any blood in my urine when I had pissed before taking my shower, so I had that going for me.

I busied myself with choking on a couple of the mini muffins, washing them down with large gulps of tepid coffee. It really was a shitty continental breakfast, and I wondered why I was bothering when I could go anywhere else in the world and do better.

And then Dolly came out of the back office, and I remembered why I was hanging around.

"Any big plans for today?" she asked brightly.

"Wandering around town and seeing the sights," I offered.

"That'll take ten minutes."

"Maybe lunch, then."

"Ooh. Don't rush yourself."

"I'm just killing time until happy hour anyway," I said.

She blushed lightly. "Oh, I have something for you," she said. She bent and opened a drawer near the floor and rummaged around inside. "Here it is," she said as she found a folded brochure. "There was a woman who stayed here last month whose husband was staying at Hidden Palms," she said. "We talked about it quite a bit. I think she was a little lonely and not quite sure what she was supposed to do, and so she was happy to have someone to talk to. I asked her about the facility, and she got me this."

The brochure was professional and filled with bright pictures of stress-free people and scenic vistas.

"Thanks," I said. "I'll give this a read."

On the back was a phone number for making appointments and other information about the Center. I tapped the number. "You don't suppose I could use the phone?" I asked.

"No need," she said. "You have an appointment at 2pm."

"I do?"

"Your personal assistant called this morning and set it up."

"She did?"

"She did."

"She's very efficient."

"You only hire the best." She gave me a bright smile.

I liked seeing that smile. "Did she use my name when making the appointment?"

"Of course." She caught the slight twitch in my mouth. "Was that bad?"

"It's fine," I said, smoothing over my momentary concern. Wilson would find out about the appointment, or he wouldn't. No point in worrying about it now. "Do I have any other appointments today?"

"As a matter of fact, you do," she said. She slipped a folded card out of the pocket of her slacks and placed it on the counter next to the brochure. "You have reservations at this restaurant at six."

I picked up the card and read the name and address printed inside. Underneath were neatly printed directions to the restaurant from the highway. It was in Santa Maria, up the road a bit from Los Alamos. "For one?" I asked.

"No," she said.

"Fancy place?"

"You don't need to wear a jacket," she said.

"How about pants?"

"Probably."

"I can manage that."

"I have no doubt that you can."

I tapped the card on the counter. "Well, I guess I know what I'm doing for the rest of the day," I said.

"I guess so," she replied.

"How about you? Any plans?"

"I'm going to be here until four," she said. "And then I'm going to go home and put on something nice."

"With pants?"

"Probably not."

"Women get all the breaks."

She leaned her elbows on the counter. "You'll thank me later," she said.

Of that, I had no doubt whatsoever.

I took the brochure to a family restaurant that served a real breakfast, and while working through two cups of hot and fresh coffee, I read the Hidden Palms Spiritual Center brochure. There was a lot to like about the Center: secluded location, a discreet and dedicated staff, twenty-plus acres of careful cultivated and managed grounds that backed up to a National Forest, a kitchen with a Michelin-rated chef and master sommelier, two pools, a private movie theater, and an laundry list of Ivy League-educated professionals.

Psychiatrists, psychologists, and behavioral scientists, oh my.

The last two pages were dedicated to the Retreat's founder and spiritual guru—Maximillian Sterling Byron III—a name which I couldn't imagine anyone saying out loud to a physician upon the arrival of said to-be-named child. The fact that it had happened three times suggested that two of the three were either total narcissists or hated their parents. I suspected the former, especially in the case of the Byron the Third, who was, in addition to being the man behind the curtain at the Center, was also an ordained minister in the First Church of the Holy Relic.

I was disappointed there wasn't any mention on the brochure of when and where one could attend services for the First Church of the Holy Relic. Nor was there any mention of which relic was the holiest one that warranted its own church, but I figured that was only revealed to those who contributed heavily to the Church and were allowed access to the inner sanctum.

There was a small picture of the minister on the last page of the brochure, along with notes that listed the numerous books written by the man himself. Titles like *Love Yourself, Be Yourself* and *Open Your Heart And Release Your Purpose.*

At first, I read that as "Release Your Porpoise," which was a much funnier book. The rest looked like the sort of New Age swill that clogged up the librarian's cart as he trundled up and down the row between the cells in prison.

Everyone had an angle, and everyone wanted to believe in something. It was human nature. We don't want to be alone, and we don't want to find out there's no real purpose to our lives. There were enough guys who embraced nihilism as a reason to wake up in the morning, and most of them ended up dead in short order. Surprised, to the very end, that believing in nothingness ended up being worth, well, not much.

I believed your day should start with a hearty breakfast, and I was delighted when the waitress brought out a heaping plate of buttermilk pancakes, eggs over easy, and fat, steaming sausage links. She refilled my coffee cup, and left me to it. I ate and thought—two activities that never got old—and watched people come and go outside the restaurant.

Los Alamos wasn't much when you were used to the endless sprawl of LA. The long valley between the San Rafael Mountains and the Pacific Ocean had been drilled and redrilled many times over since oil had first been discovered here. The relatively staid seasons meant crops like strawberries and grapes could flourish. Already there were signs that eager entrepreneurs were falling all over themselves to get into the artisanal wine-making business. And Vandenberg AFB was in the business of sending rockets into space now that there wasn't as pressing a need to send missiles across the ocean to the Soviet Union.

Somewhere in between was Lompoc, the federally-subsided country club for white-collar criminals.

A private hideaway and spiritual retreat center for ex-starlet junkies and fragile spouses of overbearing and overworked studio executives wasn't going to be out of the ordinary. Not in the slightest. Welcome to the West Coast where nothing is too strange as long as it is presented in high-definition Technicolor with 5.1 Surround Sound.

I used extra syrup on the pancakes in an effort to drown my persistence bitterness and ennui. You can take the man out of prison, but it can be hard to get prison out of the man.

After breakfast, I had a few hours to kill before I was due at Hidden Palms, and I started by driving around Los Alamos, but—like Dolly had said—that only took ten minutes, and so I ended up back on the 101.

I counted oil derricks and vineyards until I got bored with both, and got off the highway in Las Cruces, where I found a road that took me down to the ocean. I watched a couple of young men try to find tall enough waves to surf for awhile, and then I started back toward the highway.

I passed a roadside stand, selling fresh strawberries, and I stopped and bought some. I ate them while leaning against my car and watching traffic roll by. I found an antique mall, and looked at old pictures from half a century ago.

The mountains hadn't changed all that much.

I didn't see any bikers or any vehicles marked as belonging to the Santa Barbara County Sheriff's Office, which put me in a pleasant mood as I got off the 101 again at Cat Canyon and started the winding drive back toward the mountains. I stopped in Sisquoc again, where the old man remembered me. I perused his selection of sporting goods equipment, and found a couple of things that I thought might be useful over the next few days.

I loaded my purchases into the trunk, and continued up the hill to my appointment at the Hidden Palms Spiritual Center.

CHAPTER 11

I parked out of sight of the camera mounted on the gate at the Center, and walked up to the handset mounted on the wall. I was wearing the big sunglasses and baseball cap I had bought at the store in Sisquoc—the cheapest disguise in the book—and I kept my head turned away from the camera. Just in case. A woman answered the phone shortly after I picked it up, and when I said I had an appointment, she only hesitated for a second before confirming my name.

"That's right," I said.

"One moment," she said. And the moment stretched into two and then three before she came back on the line. "Very good, Mr. Bliss. Please return to your vehicle and approach the gate."

"Oh, I don't mind the walk," I said.

"Very good, sir. One moment."

I heard a click behind the gate, and the heavy barrier started to slide open.

"We'll have someone meet you at the front," the woman said.

I hung up the phone and hustled through the gate before she changed her mind.

The walk up the main road was uneventful—peaceful, even—and halfway there I was met by a slender woman in a sleek business suit that hugged her curves. She was carrying a folder marked with the logo of the Center, and she held out her hand as I approached. "Good afternoon, Mr. Bliss," she said. "My name is Natalie Davis, and I'll be happy to answer any questions you might have about the Hidden Palms Spiritual Center."

"A pleasure, Natalie," I said, giving her a polite squeeze. She wore tiny diamond studs in her ears, and there was a matching diamond nestled in the base of her throat. They all glittered like the real thing in the afternoon sun. Her nails were painted a subdued red color that matched her lipstick. She wasn't wearing any rings, and the slender face of her watch was all about minimalism over function.

"Are you looking into the Center for yourself or for . . ." She trailed off in a well-practiced fashion.

I made a play of looking around at the cottonwoods and the grounds. "If the rest of the place is as nice as this, I might want to visit myself," I said.

"You should consider it," she said. "The Hidden Palms Spiritual Center is aptly named."

"One would hope so," I said. "I suspect you wouldn't get nearly the interest if you called it 'Hayfever Hellhole and Skin Cancer Inducement Center.'"

"We strive for accuracy in our marketing," she said smoothly. "And we stay away from hyperbolic posturing."

"So, not too bad during allergy season, then?"

She inclined her head. "You are a funny man, Mr. Bliss." She said it in that chirpy way that translated to *Don't try my patience, asshole.* "What do you do for a living?"

"This and that," I said.

She wasn't nearly as impressed with that answer as Dolly had been.

"Well," she said, turning and starting to walk back toward the main house. She paused, looking over her shoulder to make sure I knew I was supposed to follow her. "The Center was founded nearly fourteen years ago by Maximillian Sterling Byron III as a sanctuary for souls who were overwhelmed by the constant pressures and calamity of modern urban living. He had found that people living in densely populated cities were statistically more inclined to psychological distress, mental maladies, and other physiological impairments that were decreasing both the quality and duration of their lives. The incessant pressure of all those people, the technology, and all those cars and trains and planes contributed to the breakdown of the mind/body connection, thereby making both the body and mind more susceptible to disease, distress, and decay."

"Sounds terrible," I said. I hurried to catch up with her and keep pace. She had a long stride, which wasn't diminished as she talked.

"Do you live in LA?" she asked.

"I do," I admitted.

"Have you lived there long?"

"Off and on over the last couple of decades," I said.

"And when you weren't living in LA, did you notice any differences in your mood? In your physical health?"

I inclined my head. "I did," I said. "But probably not for the reasons you're thinking of."

She glanced at me. "Are you suggesting that living in Los Angeles was actually better for you than other places where you've lived?"

"I'm not suggesting it," I said. "It's true."

Her brows came together. "Where were you living, Mr. Bliss?"

"Let's not dwell on that too much," I said. "Let's just pretend I agree with you that breathing all that smog every day is slowly poisoning me, okay?"

"It is, you know," she said.

I nodded, indicating that she should continue with her spiel.

"When Elder Byron first purchased this land as a spiritual haven for himself, fifteen years ago, it was a small sanctuary. During that first year, he built a one-room cabin where he could find solitude and respite from the persistence and chaos of the modern world. And once he had built his spiritual retreat, he spent another year, fasting and meditating on the purpose of existence."

We had reached the steps leading to the wide porch around the main house, and she stopped at the base of the steps. "Do you spend much time wondering why you are here, Mr. Bliss?"

"Right here?" I asked.

"Here on this planet."

"Once in a while, the question crosses my mind," I admitted.

"Is there not more to life than sitting in a car on a freeway filled with other cars, breathing all that exhaust and those chemical fumes? Are we only alive to rush to work, sit in an office for a third of our lives, rush home, and spend another third curled up in a ball underneath our sheets?"

"Well, there is that other third . . ." I reminded her.

"Is that it, then?" she asked. "Only a third of your life has value? And what do you do with it? Watch TV? Shop at the mall? Drink? Fight?" She leaned toward me, dropping her voice to a conspiratorial whisper. "Fuck?"

"There's definitely not enough of that last one going around," I said.

A fleeting smile caught in the corner of her mouth and lured me on up the steps. "We are more than mere animals. We have built immense monuments to both gods and our heroes. We have been into space, and we have seen the very deepest parts of our oceans. But we know very little about who we really are, and why we are here. The Hidden Palms Spiritual Center offers a place for you to reconnect, both with your inner self and your holistic self. *As without, as within* is our motto here."

"I'm not quite sure what that means," I admitted.

She paused at the front door of the main house, her manicured hand resting on the large bronze doorknob. "Of course not, Mr. Bliss," she said, offering me a polite but slightly condescending smile. "That's why you're here, isn't it?"

"You got me there, Natalie," I said.

She held the door for me, and I walked right on into the main house which I had walked out of yesterday under much different circumstances. As the door whispered shut behind us, I briefly glanced around, half-expecting to see the Terror Twins waiting for me. There was no one in the opulent foyer, and the room was quiet and cold.

"This way, Mr. Bliss," Natalie said as she led me to the right. The thick carpet muffled the sound of her heels, and I followed after her, feeling like I was one second away from being caught out.

But no one jumped out from behind a potted fern, and we reached a door marked "Consultations" without incident. Natalie opened the door, went in, and waited for me to follow her. I did, and she quietly shut the door behind her.

The room had several chairs and a long sofa, all finished with the same blue and gold pattern. Crystal decanters and a set of glasses sat on a wooden sideboard. A picture of a man wearing a dark red robe hung on the wall. He was standing in a garden somewhere, and a couple of birds, squirrels, and fawns were gathered around him. An expression that was half-beatific and half-stern schoolmaster glare made for an interesting expression on his face, and I wasn't quite sure if I was supposed to feel chastised or inspired by him. A tall window looked out over the grounds, and somewhere out there, I knew there was the pool where I had almost gone for a swim.

"Our illustrious founder," Natalie said, indicating the painting. "Something to drink?" she asked, her hand dropping to include the decanters.

"I feel like this is a test," I said, wandering over to the couch and sitting down. The view from the couch was worse. Now *our illustrious founder* was looking down on me.

"What kind of test?" she asked as she selected a glass from the tray.

"Would he approve?"

"Of what?"

"Of whatever you're about to pour for me," I said.

"Why would we be testing you?" she asked. She poured from one of the decanters, filling the glass half-full, and she offered it to me. "Water," she said.

"Oh," I said, and I took the glass from her. "I just assumed. What with the stoppers in those bottles that . . . you know . . ."

"It keeps the dust out," she said.

"Right," I said. What with the hermetic seal around the front door and the persistent pressure in my ears like I was underwater, I wasn't quite sure how any dust got into this place, much less collected enough to disturb a glass of water, but hey? Not my place to question the industrial design of the center, right?

I sipped from my glass, and found the water to be quite refreshing. Maybe there was something to this stoppered decanter business.

"Before we go on a tour of the grounds, Mr. Bliss, why don't you tell me a little bit about why you are interested in the center?" Natalie sat down on the couch, smoothing her skirt and sitting primly on the edge of the cushion. "I believe your assistant said something about a friend . . ."

"She did?" I gulped at the water for a second. "She did," I said again, more emphatically this time. "Yes, I'm, uh, asking for a friend, mind you."

"Of course," Natalie said smoothly. Like she'd heard this excuse a dozen times, and she probably had.

"My friend has some issues with some—shall we say—reoccurring prescriptive hazards."

"Very well."

"And what he, I mean *she*, I mean, well, anyway, some time away from the regular routine might be useful to my friend, you know?"

"I do know, Mr. Bliss. Many of our clients seek to be liberated from the constant pressure of their daily lives. It's not an uncommon malady in this age."

"Right. So, my friend wants someplace discreet. Someplace out of the way. Someplace where there won't be any judgment from the staff. Where they can just go and, you know, be peaceful for awhile."

"How long do you think your friend might be inclined to remain in a restful atmosphere that promoted peace and assisted in the release of all their built-up toxins?"

"How long does that take?"

"How long does what take?"

"The release of toxins."

"It depends on what additional programs your friend might avail themselves of during their stay."

"So there are tiers?"

"We prefer to not refer to any of our programs as *tiers*. Think of them more as *à la carte* options."

"Like when I go to the salon and get my hair cut, and then I decide to get a pedicure at the same time?"

"Exactly like that," she said smoothly.

"Could I get a pedicure here?"

"Of course."

"Do you get yours done here?"

She kicked off one of her fancy shoes. I liked how she kept her leg straight and pointed her foot as she showed off her toenails. Natalie had a lot of poise, and I had seen a few pedicures in my time. Post-prison, of course. The Chow empire included a few nail salons.

A couple of months after I had moved into the bungalow, Mrs. Chow had told me to go down and let the girls take care of me. I had insisted it wasn't necessary, and she had said okay, but a month later, she had reminded me. When I declined, the next morning a trio of giggling women had descended upon my bungalow before I had even gotten out of bed. As I tended to sleep in a rather undressed state, the sudden arrival of the trio and all their gear in my bedroom had made things extra awkward.

Afterward, I had told Mrs. Chow that I was going to get the locks changed. "Or you could just accept my gift graciously," she had said. "You'll see. The ladies will like it."

My toenails were electric blue for a couple of weeks. I wore sandals often during those weeks, and got a lot of compliments about my feet.

So what if she had been right. I still changed the locks.

"Nice," I told Natalie, and she tucked her foot back in her shoe. "How about medicated assistance with heroin withdrawal?" I asked.

"Of course," she said without missing a beat.

"Psychological counseling for pornography addiction? You know, when I—I mean, *my friend*—has difficulty relating to a real sexual partner unless one or both of them is watching porn?"

"Is that a real condition?"

"I read about it in a magazine somewhere."

"I'm sure there's an expert in the field who can be brought in for a consultation," she said.

"Really?"

She shook her head slightly, and smoothed down the front of her skirt. "Well, Mr. Bliss, do you have any more questions?"

"A few," I said.

"Okay," she said, and she clasped her hands on her knees and looked at me expectantly.

"You don't believe me," I said.

"I'm inclined to think you are wasting my time," she said.

"Was it the porn joke?"

"It didn't help."

"I do that, you know," I said. "When I get nervous."

"We all get nervous from time to time, Mr. Bliss."

"It's really difficult to admit that I have a problem. I didn't have to come here, you know."

"Of course you didn't."

"I mean, I could have gone to that other place. You know, the one, right?" I was guessing here—well, I was guessing about a lot of things—but figured the vaguer the better.

Her features tightened slightly. "Yes?"

"I mean, I hear really good things about that place. Oh, man, the list of people who have been helped there. Whew. That's some serious promotion. Even if you can't advertise it. Now, this place? I don't hear nearly the same amount of buzz about it, but—" I leaned forward, glancing up at the glaring figure of *El Illustro*. "But this place has the goods, you know?"

She was silent for a long moment, her eyes searching my face, and then she smiled again. "Very good, Mr. Bliss. I'm glad to hear that we come highly recommended."

"I really need to kick my habit," I said. "But on the hush-hush. And frankly, I've been feeling a little lost these last few months. Just not myself, you know? And yeah, yeah, I know that the drugs aren't helping, but why I'm doing them again, right? Why is that? I was clean for so long. I really thought I had it under control."

She was nodding right along with me. "I think we can do some real good for you here, Mr. Bliss. Perhaps we can even arrange from some guidance from Elder Byron himself."

"Really?" I sat up a little straighter. "You think that could happen?"

"If certain opportunities present themselves," she said smoothly, falling back into her sales pitch now. "I am certain some private sessions might be possible."

"That's fantastic," I gushed. I looked up at the picture again. "I can already tell that he wants to help me," I said.

"I hear that a lot," Natalie said. "We understand your pain. We want to help."

CHAPTER 12

Natalie and I played Questions and Answers for another half-hour or so, more questions from her than answers, but that was to be expected. We finally ran out of steam, and there wasn't much else to do but take a tour. The tour covered a lot of what I had already seen, though I did get a chance to see what one of the guest rooms looked like. Spartan. Nice view. Deadbolt on the inside of the door. Wash basin in the room. Tiny shared bathrooms with shower stalls.

As we were coming back down the main staircase, I caught sight of a familiar musclebound shape. Terrance was walking down the hall where the consultation office was, and I dallied a bit on the stairs, pretending to be interested in an enormous painting of Elder Byron that was mounted in the upper half of the grand open space that rose up from the foyer. It was similar to the one in the office, but with more birds and better lighting. God lighting, in fact.

His eyes had the same weird way of tracking you wherever you were, too.

"Well," Natalie said as we finally wandered down to the foyer again. "That's the tour. Are there any more questions, Mr. Bliss?"

A quick glance down the hall revealed no sign of Terrance. "Any chance we could take a spin around the yard?" I asked.

"No chance," she said quickly. She flashed me a bright smile. "We respect the privacy of our guests quite earnestly."

"Of course," I said.

She produced a brochure exactly like the one Dolly had given me that morning. "There are some nice pictures in this brochure," she said.

"Oh, lovely," I said, pretending to be excited about the pictures.

"Would you like to book a room now?" she asked. "And I'm sorry, was it for you or your friend?"

"Hard to say," I said. I tapped the brochure against my wrist. "Is there a discount if I book now?"

"There is no discounting of any services at the center," she said, some of that frostiness returning to her voice.

"If—sorry, *when*—I call to book a room, do I just call the number here in the brochure, or is there a better way to reach you?"

"Just tell the switchboard operator that you wish to speak with me," Natalie said. "She'll transfer you."

"Okay, great." I held out my hand. "Thanks for the tour."

"Don't mention it, Mr. Bliss." She took my hand and shook it promptly. There was no emotion on her face. Nothing to give any indication whether she was disappointed or elated that I was leaving. She had been doing cold sales like this for a long time; she was too good to let me in on what she was feeling at the moment. Though I could probably guess.

"I can let myself out," I said.

"I'll walk with you," she replied, squelching any idea I might have had about wandering off the path.

"Very well," I said. I pointed at the door, and she nodded, falling in behind me as I started toward it. "What shall we talk about on the way?"

We went out of the building and she stood on the porch for a second. "It's not that far of a walk," she pointed out. "We won't have time to talk about much."

"Baseball?" I tried. She shook her head as she started down the steps. "Deep sea fishing? Antiquing? Pugs? Squirrels? Lime Jell-O?"

She shook her head to each of them in turn, but made a face when I mentioned Jell-O. "What is there to talk about when we talk about Jell-O?" she asked.

"Whether you use gin or vodka when you make shooters."

We started walking toward the distant gate.

She made a face. "Oh, god. Vodka. Gin would taste terrible with Jell-O."

"There, see, we do have something to talk about."

"Why would anyone use gin?"

"Right? I totally agree with you. Even better might be some sort of white rum."

"Whoever invented this concoction?"

"You've never had a Jell-O shooter?"

"No. I can't say that I have."

"How about a Long Island Iced Tea? Or a Mai Tai?"

"I don't know what those are, sorry."

"Do you even drink? I supposed I should have asked before I went plowing ahead like this."

She laughed. "I do, but rarely."

"Why not? No friends?"

"I have friends."

"But they don't drink."

"No, they do. It's just . . . it's much more . . . social drinking."

"Of course it is. Otherwise dealing with other people would be intolerable, right?"

"Do you have any friends, Mr. Bliss?"

"At least one," I said. I smiled at her.

"Any other friends?"

"A couple."

"And do they drink?"

"Of course they do. I wouldn't be their friends otherwise."

"And that's how you define your friendship with these people?" Natalie asked. "By whether or not they'll drink with you?"

"No, we usually drink after sex. Or after we've hidden the body. Sometimes both."

"In that order?" she asked.

"Which order?"

"Hiding the body. Sex. And then drinking."

I nodded. "Yeah, mostly."

She stopped walking. We were about three quarters of the way to the gate. "It's been an interesting interview, Mr. Bliss," she said. She held out her hand one more time. I took it, and smiled at her as we shook hands. "Good afternoon, sir."

"Good afternoon, Natalie," I said.

"I hope we'll hear from you soon."

"Me too."

She nodded toward the gate. "I'll have it opened when you get there," she said.

"Okay." I let go of her hand and stood there awkwardly for a minute, and then I nodded. That was that. "All done," I said.

"All done," she said.

"I feel like I should offer to kiss you on the cheek or something," I started.

"Please don't," she said.

"But we haven't hidden a body together yet, so that's probably a little premature in our friendship."

She cocked an eyebrow at me, and with a tiny smile on her lips, she turned and started back toward the house. I stood there for a while, watching her hips move back and forth, and I was pretty sure she knew I was watching. When she got to the main porch, I let out a tiny sigh and raised my hand to wave goodbye.

She waved back, and behind me, I heard the gate motor start running.

I walked straight out. Rocking my hips a bit too.

Two can play that game.

I still wasn't any closer to finding Gloria, and short of checking myself into the center, I wasn't sure of any other way to find out if she was there without alerting Wilson and his goons. And maybe it would come to that, but that wasn't a problem I had to solve this afternoon.

My dinner reservation wasn't for a few hours yet, and so I drove north from Hidden Palms instead of south and ended up at the interchange for 166. I turned left, and merged onto the highway. It would wind its way back across the mountains to Santa Maria. It was out of my way, but it gave me time to think.

Mid-week traffic was light, and overhead, wispy clouds stretched across the pale sky. The hills were covered with a mix of cotton-woods, pine, and oak, creating a patterned layer of yellow and green. It was good to get away from both the coast and the city. Not quite lost in nature, but far enough out that there wasn't an omnipresent reminder of our presence on this planet.

I wasn't much for philosophical musings about the grander scheme of things, and if I had spent a year in the woods, meditating on the ultimate purpose of our lives, I'm sure I might be more inclined to such thinking on a regular basis. I had had a lot of time to think over the last decade or so, and some of it was actually in relative solitude. But I had been surrounded by concrete and steel, confined to a space not much larger than the inside of my car. Such incarceration tended to focus your mind on more physical world issues. For a time, though. After a few years, you learned how to survive. How to keep your sanity.

Some of the inmates had been very regimented about it. They weren't going to let prison change them. They built walls within the walls, and kept precise count of the number of days they had left before they left the state-made walls behind. When their release days arrived, they marched out of the block without so much as a glance back. I wondered about them sometimes. I wondered if their walls had been successful at keeping their true selves safe from prison, and if they had been able to tear down those walls they had made for themselves.

I wasn't sure I could live by myself in the woods. It would be too much like solitary. I knew the city. I knew that constant pressure of other people—other lives—around you. It was comforting to know you were surrounded by others who were just like you. Some of them were more caged than others, but we were all part of a community, our cellblocks demarcated by the highways that criss-crossed LA.

Shortly after I passed a sign for a recreation area at a mountain lake, I caught sight of urban sprawl between two hills that didn't quite touch. The sky lost some of its color as my car dropped down into the valley once more, and the grid of Santa Maria's streets stretched out before me.

I picked up the card that Dolly had given me. The name and address of the restaurant were written on the back. I had about an hour to find the place. Putting aside the introspective mood that the drive had brought up, I started paying attention to the exit signs, trying to figure out which was the best one to help me find the restaurant.

The restaurant was called Ambrosia, and its sign featured a trio of comically drawn fauns pouring wine into a large bowl of grapes and apples and other fruit. The decor inside was variations on that theme, and long drapes of red and purple covered much of the old wood of the walls. The tables were small, lit by arrangements of tiny candles, and there was an upstairs loft that was framed in with bookcases. Beneath the loft was the bar and the floor-to-ceiling cases of the wine cellar, and it looked like they had an extensive selection.

I was early, and the hostess said I could sit in the bar until the rest of my party arrived. I glanced around at all the empty tables in the restaurant proper, but didn't bother to quibble with their process. They undoubtedly had an image to maintain, and someone thought that men sitting by themselves at romantically lit tables probably wasn't as enticing for business as dudes swiveling around on bar stools so they could check out the room.

Because that's what we do when we're stuck in the bar.

The bartender slipped a long menu filled with signature cocktails, stood there for a minute with a bored look on his face, and when it was apparent I was going to read the whole thing, he wandered off. I almost called him back and ordered something at random, but I wasn't in that much of a rush to start drinking.

I nursed my water and, as you might expect, swiveled around on my seat to check out the room.

This wasn't the kind of place that did happy hour for the downtown professional set. They opened for dinner at five, and expected most of their reservations to show up at seven or later. There was probably a late evening crowd as well, but most likely, everyone went home by eleven. It was a short work day, and judging from the measured pace of the staff, they all knew exactly how busy they were going to be on any given night. There weren't many surprises at Ambrosia, and the tips were good and solid.

It's good to be a gastronomical landmark. You're always there. Your food and service are always excellent. You don't try new things to entice new markets. You open; you foster a romantic and enjoyable atmosphere for your customers; you clean up and go home: what wasn't to love about that? Purpose and consistency. Many never had that in their lives, and those who found it, tended to hang on to it, because they knew how fortunate they were.

Upon my release from Tehachapi, the highlights of my résumé were *ex-con* and *ex-porn star*. One of the only real jobs I had been able to find—after a year or so of willfully ignoring the reality of my job qualifications while the rest of the world didn't—was *Tire Buffer* at Speedy's Car Wash in West Hollywood. I was the guy who polished the chrome on the rims of the HumVees, BMWs, Mercedes-Benzes, and tricked-out SUVs who rolled through the wash.

I was not the guy who vacuumed, nor the guy who did windows. Nor was I the guy who polished rearview mirrors and opened car doors for the customers. He was the one who got the tips. That money was supposed to be evenly split between us, but door guy had been pinched for shoplifting once or twice as a juvie and he had quick fingers.

He had had an accident in the break room one afternoon. Busted his wrist trying to get a soda out of the machine. The rest of us were sorry to see him go, but the split was much better after that.

That lasted for three months, and then West Hollywood Vice raided the place and shut it down. Apparently, there was a spot during the car wash cycle when the vehicle wasn't visible from the street—which wasn't unusual in and of itself—but during this part of the wash, drugs could be stashed in and taken out of the cars. Who knew? I certainly hadn't. I found out about it in the paper the following week.

And the only reason I hadn't gone to work that day was because Mr. Chow had called the night before to tell me he was out of prison. He had insisted that I come visit him at his house in Venice the next day. *I have to work*, I had told him.

Fuck that job, he had said. *It is beneath you. Crawling around on your hands and knees in an inch of water that is filled with chemicals that will rot your guts.*

You have something better in mind?

Of course I do.

I missed the raid because Mr. Chow wanted me to take his wife shopping in Beverly Hills.

Three months later, the cancer took him. And I continued to take Mrs. Chow shopping.

Purpose and consistency. The two things that hold the universe together.

CHAPTER 13

DOLLY SWEPT IN RIGHT AT SIX, WEARING A SLEEVELESS DRESS THAT showed off her upper arms and clavicle. It was dark blue, tailored at the waist, and it fell loosely to just above her knees. She was wearing block-heeled sandals the same color as her hair, which was loose about her shoulders. She could look me in the eye as I sat on the barstool, and she laid her hand lightly on my arm as she reached me.

"Hi," she said. A little breathlessly. But not so much that I thought she had been running to get here in time. More that she was excited to see me.

"Hi," I said back. Not quite as breathlessly, but still quite excited.

A waiter carrying a large tray crossed behind her, and she stepped forward to get out of his way. My knees brushed her skirt.

"We should tell them you're here," I said, after taking a moment to compose myself.

"I did," she said. She looked at the nearly empty glass on the bar. "What's that?"

"Manhattan," I said. I offered her the glass, and her fingers brushed mine as she took the glass. "It's basically bourbon, vermouth, and bitters, but every bar has its own twist. You can tell a lot about a bartender by how they make a Manhattan. Or by how they make a martini. Or—well, there are a couple of ways you can tell."

She took a tiny sip. "It's nice," she said. "Orangey."

"That's not a word."

"It's a flavor," she countered.

"Fine. Like 'lemony'?"

"And 'minty,'" she said.

"There we go, then. *Orangey* it is."

I looked at the glass, and she smiled as she raised it to her mouth. "Oh, you're not getting this back," she said.

I was going to protest, but I liked watching her drink. She leaned forward, and her shoulder brushed against me as she set the glass down on the bar. "Are you going to order me another one, Bliss, or is there something else I should try?"

"A glass of wine?" I suggested.

"I'm not in the mood for wine tonight," she said.

The hostess hovered nearby, derailing my thought train. "Your table is ready," she said.

Dolly smiled at me, and turned smartly and followed the young woman toward one of the small tables. I slipped a twenty off my clip, tossed it on the bar, and followed Dolly in her blue dress.

Our table was against the wall, and a long drape of dark purple fabric covered the wall to our left. The table was small enough that our knees brushed without much effort, and once we were settled, Dolly leaned her leg against mine.

"Worried I might run away?" I asked.

"I don't want you to step on my toes. You have large feet, and those boots . . ."

"What's wrong with my boots?"

"They're, like, ten years out of style."

"They're comfortable."

"So are sweat pants, but that doesn't mean you should wear them in public."

"These are leather. It takes awhile for good shoes to break in. To really fit your feet. That's when they stop feeling like you've shoved your feet into wet cement. It's all about comfort and support."

"I have a bra that *totally* fits that description. But do you see me wearing it tonight?"

"I don't know. Are you?"

"It doesn't match this dress, for one thing."

"How would I know?"

"I would know." She leaned forward, her voice dropping to a whisper. "The one I'm wearing right now?"

I leaned forward too. "Yes?"

"Matching panties."

"Really?"

She nodded as if I had just confirmed that yes, indeed, the sun did rise in the east and set in the west.

"My socks match my briefs," I said.

"Not white, I hope."

"You don't like white briefs?"

"I don't want to imagine you wearing white socks with those boots."

"Give me a little credit," I said. "Besides, maybe I'm not wearing any socks at all."

It took her a second to get that, and then she laughed, wrinkling her nose and sitting back in her chair. Her leg pressed against mine.

Her laugh and body motion startled the young waiter who had just arrived at our table. "Oh, uh, good evening," he said. "My name is Julio. I'll be your server this evening. And how are you two tonight?"

"I'm good," I said. I glanced at Dolly. "You? Are you good?"

Dolly's shoulders were still shivering with laughter, and she held her hand in front of her mouth. She managed to nod.

"We're good," I said.

"Can I tell you about our specials tonight?" our waiter asked.

Dolly managed to get her amusement under control, and she lowered her hand. "Do your socks match your briefs?" she asked Julio.

"Excuse me?"

"It's not quite the same thing as asking if the carpets match the drapes, if you know what I mean," I explained. That only set Dolly off again.

"I . . . I don't understand," Julio said. "Is this . . . ?"

"I'm not wearing any socks," I said.

"What . . . What does that mean?"

"It means I'm not wearing any, you know."

He shook his head. "No, I . . . I don't know."

"Well, you'll figure it out someday, I hope."

Dolly let out a small shriek of laughter.

Julio tried again. "Would you like to hear about tonight's specials?"

I shook my head. "Not right now. How about you bring us one of the house Manhattans and a Vieux Carré. The bartender know how to make one of those?"

"I'll . . . I'll ask."

"Great. Thanks, Julio." After he was gone, I leaned forward to whisper to Dolly, "I am actually wearing socks. And they're not white."

She leaned forward too, and moved aside the fabric of her dress from her left shoulder. "I'm not wearing white, either," she said. What she was wearing under the dress was several shades darker. And silky.

"Oh, my," I said.

Dolly sat back in her chair, her smile suggesting she was pleased with my response. She picked up the paper menu and perused it. "Someone called the hotel today," she said. "Asking for you."

"For me? By name?"

She nodded.

"Did they say why?"

"No," she said.

"Did you tell them I was staying there?"

"Not really."

"That's not quite the same thing as 'no,'" I pointed out.

She glanced at me over the top of her menu. "It has more letters," she said.

"And tends to mean something like 'Well, I don't want to outright lie to you, but I'd rather not tell you the truth either, and so we'll wander into this sort of vague terrain in the middle where I have some deniability later if it comes back to bite me on the ass.'"

"It's not like that," she said.

"So, the answer is, actually, 'no.'"

She hesitated for a minute. "Not really," she said.

"What did you say, Dolly?"

"I didn't say anything," she said defensively. "I answered the phone, like I always do, and a woman asked if you were staying there. I told her I couldn't give out that information, but that I could take a message."

"Isn't that confirming that I am actually staying there?"

"No," she said. "Desk clerks do it all the time. We just say 'uh-huh' a lot while they're leaving the message, and then we say, 'Okay, if that person ever checks in here, we'll give them that message.' And they usually get the hint."

"Did this person leave a message?"

"She said she'd call back tomorrow."

"And all desk clerks do this? So if I called fifty hotels and asked if I was staying there at each of them, all the clerks would take a message and not write it down. And then tell me that silliness about me checking in some day?"

"Some of them would, yes."

"But not all of them?"

She lifted her shoulders. "Probably?"

"So, like what? Thirty percent? Twenty-five?"

"Sure . . ."

"So if I called four hotels, and only one of them did this, and the others outright said 'He's not staying here,' might that not lead me to the conclusion that the hotel where someone actually took a message might actually be the hotel I was staying at?"

"Maybe . . . ?"

I sighed.

"Are you mad at me?"

I shook my head.

"She said she'd call back tomorrow," Dolly offered, her voice getting smaller.

"It's fine," I said. "Really."

"Does that mean you have to check out? Tonight?"

"What? No, of course not. It's okay, Dolly. It really is."

The only woman who had any idea where I might be was Babs. Or her sister. Either one calling only meant Matesson was asking about my progress. I didn't have much to tell him (or them), and so any conversation we were going to have tomorrow would be pretty short. I didn't recall telling Babs where I was staying in Los Alamos, but maybe the name of the hotel showed up on Caller ID or something.

Julio returned with two drinks, which he carefully put down on the table. He put the Manhattan in front of me and the Vieux Carré in front of Dolly. "Here we go," he said, pleased with himself.

I reached over and picked up the Vieux Carré. His face fell, but I took a sip and pronounced it delightful, which brought his smile back.

"Now, for our specials—"

"Oh, dear," Dolly said. "We haven't had a chance to even think about food yet. Can we have a minute or two to try these drinks and look at the menu?"

"I, uh, sure." Julio hesitated, not quite sure which direction he should go, and then his brain made a decision for him, and directed him back toward the bar.

Dolly set her menu aside and reached for the drink in my hand.

"Oh no," I said, taking it out of reach. "This one is mine."

She made a face and picked up the Manhattan. "Is this the same thing as what you were drinking at the bar?" she asked.

"It is."

She took a sip.

"That was kind of mean," I said. "What you did to poor Julio."

"He's a hoverer," she said. "I can tell. He needs to give us some space."

"Are we going to be here awhile?"

"Maybe," she said, a merry twinkle in her eye.

I put my glass forward to toast to that, and she snatched it out of my grasp. Only a little bit sloshed onto her hand.

"Hey," I protested.

She held both glasses close to her breasts. "Mine," she said.

"Don't make me come over there," I said.

"Please do," she said. Without breaking eye contact, she lifted my drink to her lips and sipped slowly.

I vibrated my leg under the table, making it dance a bit, and she jumped slightly and then laughed at her surprise. "What are you doing?"

"I'm getting ready to come over there."

"Starting your engines, are you?"

"Vroom, vroom," I said, making the table shiver again.

Her eyes were bright, and her smile was big. "I like the sound of your engine," she said.

Eventually, we let Julio tell us about the specials. Dolly went with the fish, and as I was partial to animals that stuck to dry land, I went with the chicken. We ordered another round of drinks too, and while we waited for them, I told Dolly about my visit to Hidden Palms.

"Did you see your friend?"

"They weren't too keen on letting me wander around and pester the guests."

"I suppose not. It is a private resort, after all, isn't it?"

"A resort? I thought it was a spiritual center?"

"Can't it be both?" she asked.

"I don't get the sense that Hidden Palms is working hard to get listed in Zagat's."

"One of the rumors I was going to tell you about was that I heard it was a place for high-profile Hollywood types to kick bad habits."

"I definitely got that sense," I said.

"Is that why your friend is there?"

"Gloria?" I shook my head. "I don't know really. Probably."

"You don't know?"

"We haven't kept up."

"So why are you looking for her?"

"Another friend asked me to."

"So you are a bounty hunter," she said, pleased to have caught me out.

"No, I'm not. I just . . . I'm looking for a friend for another friend. That's all."

"Is the friend paying you?"

"Sort of . . ."

"That's kind of like 'not really,'" she said.

"Okay, fine. Yes. He's paying me. I'm tracking her down. It's just like that. But, also, I did know her. One upon a time."

"What happened?"

"You are full of questions," I said.

"I'm actually getting answers, so why shouldn't I be?" was her response.

I was spared any further interrogation by Julio's return. He put two more drinks on the table, as well as two small dishes that each had a tiny pastry augmented with a dollop of white sauce and a mint leaf. "Compliments of the chef," he said.

"Do we know the chef?" I asked, staring somewhat dubiously at the mystery pastry.

"Chef Roberto Achellini?"

I looked at Dolly, who shrugged.

"So if we don't know him, why is he sending food out to our table?"

"You're kidding me, right?" Julio asked.

"About what?"

He glanced around the room. "We bring out one of these for everyone. That's just what I'm supposed to say."

"So it's not really compliments of the 'chef,' is it?" I pointed out. "It's more like, 'hey, here's a pastry on the house.' What? You don't do free bread anymore?"

"We never did free bread," Julio said.

I looked at Dolly. "I can't believe you picked a place that doesn't do free bread," I said.

She toasted Julio with her drink. "Drinks are good, though," she said. "You can get a loaf of bread at Ralph's on the way home."

"You can," Julio said.

"Why are you siding with her?" I asked.

He put up his hands and backed away. "Hey, man, I'm just trying—" He didn't even bother finishing; he just turned and bolted.

"You are so mean," Dolly said.

"You helped."

She pouted a little bit. "I did. Does that make me a bad girl?"

I nearly choked on my drink.

"I'll take that as a 'yes,'" she said with a smile.

I got my breathing under control, and then took a proper sip from my drink to show that I had everything under control. Her leg was rubbing against mine in that comfortable way people get after a few drinks. I was sort of hoping she'd show me her bra strap again. Maybe I'd ask politely.

"What kind of drugs?" she asked suddenly.

"Gloria?" I shook my head. "I don't know."

"No," she said. "You. You said you went to prison for drugs. What kind?"

"Did I?"

"You did."

"I did."

"What kind?" she asked again.

"Do you really want to know?" I tried to deflect her question.

She nodded slowly, letting me know she was serious. But her leg had stopped its motion, and she took a long sip from her drink as she waited for me to respond.

"Cocaine," I said. "It wasn't enough that I had some, but I got sent up for possession, intent to sell, and transporting it."

"Were you? What do they call it? A mule? Were you a mule?"

"I was not a mule. I was barely a recreational user."

"The drugs just happened to be in your car when the cops pulled you over?"

"It wasn't my car, and no, the cops didn't pull me over."

"Did you steal the wrong guy's car?"

"No, I didn't steal the car," I said.

"So why did you do it?"

"I didn't." I paused and sighed. "It's a long story," I said.

"Sordid?"

"Terribly."

"Is it going to make me think less of you?"

"Probably."

She thought about that for a second. "Well," she decided, "I'll leave that for tomorrow then. I would like to think highly of you for a few hours yet."

"Excellent," I said, lifting my glass. "I like that idea."

"So what did you do before you weren't riding around in a car that wasn't yours with a bunch of drugs that you don't know how they got there?"

I drank heavily from my glass. "Where is our food?" I asked, looking around for Julio.

The food, when it arrived and spared me further embarrassment, was delicious. We continued to talk about everything and nothing, laughing more often than not. Finding excuses to touch more often than not. Our legs, pressing against one another. Moving apart, and coming back again. Her lips, lingering on the rim of her glass. Her eyes, watching me.

By the time Julio had cleared the plates and was working on getting us after-dinner coffees, I was ready to sweep the decorative candles off the table and climb over it and kiss her. Judging by the look in her eye, she was hoping I would.

Julio cleared his throat, and I pulled my gaze away from Dolly's face. "Would you like to see a dessert menu?" he asked.

"If it's more complicated than pudding in a cup that is ready to serve right now, then no," I said.

Julio looked at Dolly, who shook her head politely. He may have rolled his eyes slightly as he walked off.

I started toying with the edge of the decorative display, sliding it back and forth an inch or so.

A phone rang somewhere close by. Dolly's eyebrows pinched together, and her lips firmed.

"Is that . . . ?" I asked.

"It's my cellphone," she said.

We listened to it ring twice more.

"Shouldn't you answer that?" I asked.

"They'll leave a message," she said, and the phone stopped ringing. "See?" she said.

Ten seconds later, it started ringing again.

"I'm sorry," she said, reaching for her tiny purse. "It's probably Rick, at the hotel. This'll just be a second."

"It's no problem," I said.

She found her tiny flip phone in her purse, and a puzzled expression crossed her face when she looked at the display. She flipped the phone open and put it to her ear.

"Hello?" she said. "Yes, this is she. Uh, okay."

She glanced at me, and there was something in her eyes that I hadn't seen all evening.

"Yes," she said, breathlessly returning her attention to the phone. "David? What's going on?" She listened intently, her eyes tracking back and forth. "My God," she muttered. "You didn't. Oh my God, David. No." She put her hand over her mouth, fighting back some emotion that threatened to spill out of her.

"No," she said sternly in response to something said to her. "I am not calling Mom. Just—no, damnit. David. We talked about this. You were supposed—" Her lips made a tight line and she shook her head slowly as she listened. "I'll be there," she interrupted. "I'm coming down there now. No! I'm coming down."

She hung up the phone before anything else could be said, and then she put her head in her hands. Her shoulders shook as she drew in a long breath. She dropped her hands to the table, and raised her face to me. Her eyes were bright with tears. "I have to go," she said in a tiny voice.

"What is it?" I asked.

She shook her head. "I'm sorry, Bliss. I'm so sorry."

She stuffed her phone in her purse as she pushed her chair back from the table.

I started to get up too, but she shook her head, telling me to stay put. She stood next to the table for a second, wiping at the corner of her eye.

"This was really nice," she said in a quiet voice, and when I reached out for her arm, she fled.

I was utterly confused about what had just happened.

Someone made a noise, and I realized Julio was standing awkwardly nearby. "It was the underwear thing, wasn't it?" he asked. "That's what wrecked it, wasn't it?"

"It was not the underwear thing," I said. "She just had an important meeting she forgot about."

"Uh-huh," he said.

"Do you want a tip or not?" My voice was harder than I meant it to be.

He shrugged. "She told us to put the whole meal on her credit card when she made the reservation," he said.

"You can do that?"

"She did."

"She's clever," I said softly.

Julio pressed his lips together and raised his eyebrows.

"Well, bring me the bill anyway," I said, waving a hand in his direction. I was suddenly very tired. "Maybe I'll pay it again, just because you've been a good sport."

"Very good, sir," he said.

"Did she leave a phone number when she made her reservation?" I asked, not willing to give up quite yet.

He hesitated for half a second. "I'll check," he said.

"Now I'm definitely leaving a tip," I said.

I stared at the door of the restaurant, willing it to open and let her back in. Wishing the last few minutes hadn't happened. Was there something I could have done that would have prevented that call from coming in?

She had called him David and had said "Mom." Her brother had done something stupid. He only got one phone call, and he had used it to call his big sister.

I don't remember who I had called when I had been arrested. Maybe I hadn't called anyone. If I had, it hadn't made any difference. I hadn't had a big sister like Dolly. I had been on my own.

Which meant I didn't blame her in the slightest for leaving me in the restaurant.

And then it sank in that I was still alone, after all these years.

CHAPTER 14

I DIDN'T HAVE MUCH ELSE TO DO, WHAT WITH THE ABRUPT END to dinner, and so I drove back to Los Alamos and the hotel. I went up to my room, noted the curtains were as I had left them, and cautiously went in. No one was waiting for me, and so I used the phone in the room to call the number I had gotten from Julio. It rang a few times, before a recording of Dolly's voice told me to leave a message after the tone.

"Hi," I said, when I was prompted to speak. "It's me. I'm sorry about whatever it is that's going on. Not that I had anything to do with it, really. I don't know why I said that, I guess, I . . . I guess I'm just sorry that whatever happened has happened. Anyway, I just wanted to call and say that dinner was great, and the company was better, and I hope we can do it again some time. And—"

Whatever machine was on the other end beeped suddenly, cutting me off.

I stood there for a second, phone in my hand, feeling like an idiot as I replayed what I had said. I almost called her back and tried again.

I sat on the end of the bed for a few minutes, staring at the phone, and it didn't ring.

I stretched out and stared at the ceiling for awhile.

The phone still didn't ring.

I got up, and went and used the bathroom. Washed my hands. And came back and sat down on the bed again.

The phone still didn't ring.

I left the hotel room.

Waiting on the inside was a Zen exercise. Waiting on the outside was excruciating. When you're in a cell, you have nowhere else to go. No other appointments you need to keep. It's easy to learn how to wait in prison. An hour is nothing when you have months and years before you get out. A week is barely enough time to get worked up about anything.

There was a sliver of moon in the sky, hanging low and brushing the tops of the mountains. The air was cool and gentle on my face. I decided to walk over to Rye. Just in case the sheriff's deputy was looking for an excuse to get inside my car. And as I walked, I put aside the notion of waiting for the phone to ring, and thought about my other problem.

By the time I reached Rye, I was thinking about delivery trucks. Maybe that was the key to getting into Hidden Palms. Not by hanging off the back bumper, but by being inside the truck. I just had to convince the deliverymen to let me go for a ride.

There were a handful of cars in the lot, and I circled around to the back of the restaurant. The beer garden was empty, and the French doors were shut. There wasn't much else at the back other than an old chair next to an ashtray and a couple of locked dumpsters. I sat on the chair and listened to the distant thump of noise from the restaurant. The lights from the parking lot left a lot of shadows, and if I leaned back in the chair, I was almost lost in the night.

Finally, the kitchen door opened and a figure came out. He didn't see me at first, too busy fishing underneath his apron for a lighter. When he found it and flicked it on, I caught sight of a heavily lined and bearded face, and a fat, hand-rolled spliff shoved between his lips. He saw me too, and almost dropped his marijuana cigarette. The tiny flame went out as he juggled his weed and the lighter. Wisely, he opted to hang on to his fattie, and the lighter clattered on the concrete.

"Jesus Christ," he swore. "What the fuck?"

I spotted the lighter and picked it up. It was an old metal Zippo, and I flicked it with my thumb to bring the flame. He took the lighter back, lit his spliff, and then snapped the metal case closed. He held in his marijuana smoke for a moment, and then exhaled noisily, blowing the smoke in my direction.

"What the fuck?" he asked again.

"Sorry," I said. "It seemed like a quiet spot."

"Do I know you?" His voice sounded like tires crunching on an old gravel road, and the light from his hand-rolled made his face even craggier.

"I doubt it," I said. "I was here the other night. Had a few drinks. You watched me have a chat with local law enforcement."

"That's right," he said.

"That was Deputy Dawg, right?"

He laughed, a noise like stones turning over in a washing machine. "Hackman," he said. "Deputy Franklin Hackman. One of Santa Barbara's County's finest."

"You don't seem like a fan," I said.

He took a long drag on his spliff, and the pungent odor of his weed swirled around us as it crackled and burned. "Not sure what it matters to you," he said.

"It probably doesn't," I said, crossing my arms and leaning back in the chair again. "Just curious."

"I was curious once," he said.

"What happened."

"Tet."

"What?"

"The Tet Offensive," he said. "'Nam. '68."

"Before my time," I said.

He inhaled again, and when he exhaled, he directed the plume of smoke away from me. "I'm not going to share," he said.

"I'm good with the secondhand buzz," I said.

"Why was Hack busting your balls?" he asked.

"I suspect he does it with a lot of people," I said.

He shrugged. "Especially those who've got that look."

"Which look is that?"

"The one you get from squinting through bars."

"Ah, that one."

I checked his arms, and while it was too dim to see any details, I spotted a couple of blobs on his right arm. Military tats. Not the stuff you got in prison. "After you got back?" I asked.

"Yeah," he said. "Did a nickel in Lewisburg."

"For stupid shit?"

"Isn't it always?"

"I did a pair of nickels at Tehachapi," I said.

He laughed. "A pair?"

"Went in with one; ended up with two," I explained.

"Went back for a second helping of stupid, did you?"

"That's a pretty good way to put it," I said.

His spliff was more than halfway gone, and he hesitated for a second as he raised it to his lips again.

I waved him off. We might be best pals now, but I didn't need him to feel like he had to share.

"What's on your mind, friend?" he asked after exhaling another lungful of marijuana smoke. "You ain't sitting out here for the atmosphere."

"I was hoping to have a chat with you," I said.

"Chat away. I've got a few minutes left on my state-mandated break."

"There's a delivery truck that was here yesterday. A white one—"

His mood changed abruptly. "Ah, man," he said as he pinched the end of his spliff, putting out the smoldering weed.

"What?" I asked.

"Go fuck yourself," he said.

While I was wondering what had set him off, he went back into the restaurant and closed the door firmly behind him.

A few minutes later, before the sweet secondhand smoke buzz was gone, an SUV turned into the lot. It swung around, its high beams blinding me. The car came to a sudden stop, and I blinked heavily, trying to see through the spots dancing on my retinas. I heard the car door slam, and as my vision finally cooperated, I looked up at a familiar flat-brimmed hat.

"Well, shit," I said.

"Get up," said Deputy Franklin Hackman. "Turn around, and put your face against the wall with your hands behind your back."

"What for?" I asked.

His hand dropped to the butt of his service weapon, and my hands went up. "I'm complying," I said. I stood up and turned around. He shoved me against the wall, and pulled one arm and then the other down behind my back. I felt the cold metal of his handcuffs close around my wrists.

He walked back to his SUV, hauling me with him. I stumbled backward, trying not to fall down. He opened the back passenger side door, spun me around, and shoved me. I narrowly escaped banging my head on the door frame, as I sprawled into the car. He shoved my feet in, slammed the door, and then got into the driver's seat. I struggled to sit up as he started the car, put it in reverse, and backed up.

He sped out of the parking lot, bouncing hard across the curb, and I rolled around like a gerbil in a habitrail during an earthquake. I made some noises as I struggled to sit upright without having to sit on my hands.

His eyes flicked up toward the rearview mirror, checking on me. "We need to talk," he said.

Those certainly weren't the words I had been expecting to come out of his mouth. "Sure," I replied. "Let's talk."

What else was I going to say?

CHAPTER 15

HACK DROVE FOR A FEW MORE BLOCKS AND FINALLY TURNED INTO an empty lot near a long warehouse. He pulled around to the side of the building and stopped the car. He took off his hat and looked back at me through the grating. "I'm going to get out, and then I'm going to get you out. Okay?"

"Works for me," I said.

That was pretty much how it went. Once I was out of the SUV, he pushed me up against the side as he pulled at the handcuffs. I felt him remove the cuff on one hand, and when I tensed, he jerked my other arm up. "Hold still," he hissed. He didn't bother unlocking the other cuff though, and with a shove, he backed away from me.

I remained still, chest pressed against the car, and after a few seconds, I slowly turned my head, trying to find him in the gloom. There were no lights in the warehouse or in the lot. The only illumination was coming from the thin moon, which hung nervously in the sky to my right.

"I'm going to assume you're not going to shoot me while I'm leaning against your car," I said.

"I'm not," Hack said. "You can turn around."

I did, keeping my back to the car. I let my fingers explore the handcuff still attached to my left wrist. I knew how to get out of them—one of the useful skills you pick up while incarcerated—but I had one hand free, and the remaining cuff wasn't too tight.

He was about fifteen feet away from me, not much more than a man-shaped blob in the dark. I could hear his breathing, loud and nervous.

"I'm listening," I said.

"You were supposed to make contact with me," he said. "Not doing whatever the fuck it is you're doing."

101

I looked over at the moon again as if it could offer some insight into what Deputy Hackman was talking about. "I was getting the lay of the land," I said, playing for time.

"Goddamn it. It's my ass on the line here," he snapped. "I've been calling you for months now, and—look, I handed you this whole thing. All you needed to—"

"What's happened?" I asked. I didn't want to interrupt him, but at the same time, the longer he ran at the mouth, the more thinking out loud he'd be doing, and I had a feeling now was not the time for a lot of introspection. *Keep moving. Don't stand still.*

"The kid—David Boreal—got picked up."

The name didn't ring any bells, but then I remembered Dolly's conversation at the restaurant, and then pieces started to fall into place. *David Boreal.* Dolly's perpetually pot-addled brother.

"Where?" I asked.

"Oceano. Outside the SVRA, thank God."

"What was he doing?"

"Selling weed, the dumb fuck. He had bags of it in his van."

I hesitated, not quite sure of what to say. From an ex-con's perspective, getting caught selling was bad news, but from SBCSO's side of the law, busting a dealer with a van full of baggies was a score. So why was Deputy Hackman all stressed out?

Unless, the Santa Barbara County Sheriff's Office was involved in some way and . . .

"You don't have him," I said.

"No shit, I don't. He's at the Santa Maria Branch jail. They're going to process him in the morning. Probably transfer him to County after that. Unless we can get him out."

"We?"

"Yeah, you and I. And . . ." He didn't move much, but I could feel a change in his demeanor. The wheels in his head were churning. He was starting to think too much. "How do I know—"

"Seriously?" I interjected. "You think I'm carrying ID on me?" I didn't know who I was supposed to be, but I had an idea. Not much of one, mind you, but enough to push back. Bluff my way out. "I'm undercover, you idiot. Why do you think I was driving around like a fucking tourist? And that bullshit you pulled on me last night in the parking lot? That wasn't smart."

"What bullshit? What?"

"Following me from the restaurant. Accosting me in the parking lot. In front of witnesses, even."

"Last night?"

It was almost as if he didn't remember. Seriously?

"Look, it's not important now," I said. "We have bigger problems, don't we?" He didn't respond right away—those wheels were making a lot of noise in his head—and so I pressed him. "Don't we?"

He undid the strap over his service weapon. "Tell me something about citrus farming," he said. "Something I don't know."

"It's fucking California," I said. "We're number two after Florida. What is this? Agriculture Hour? You want some hot tips about whatever it is they do to oranges to make them grow?"

"Grafting," he said. "They graft a bud onto rootstock, so that they can control what type of orange they grow."

"Probably the same sort of shit they do with weed," I said. "Who knows? Do I look like I have a degree in biology?"

We shared a tense moment in the moonlight, and then he exhaled loudly.

I did too, but I kept it quiet.

"Look," I said, raising my hands so he could see I wasn't doing anything funny with them. The clicking noise of the open handcuff against the chain caught his attention. "Do we have a problem or not? Do you want to fix it or not?"

"God damnit," he said. "Okay, okay." He exhaled loudly again, and I wondered if he was going to hyperventilate on me. "Look, when I first called your offices and said I wanted to cut a deal, your people said they'd look into it. I called back a month later, and told them that if they wanted this whole region delivered to them, that I was their man. Not just the weed. I could deliver the whole cocaine supply chain, up and down the 101. And some jackass middle manager said they'd look into it. Again.

"And when I called last week, I told them to send someone out, someone I could talk to. I gave you—fuck! I gave you evidence that could get me in some serious trouble. And who did they send? Some asshole who wants to wander around and get acclimated to the environment or some shit. Well, tourist time is over, Bliss. Boreal is in lockup. When they transfer him to County, the crazy mother-fuckers are going to have him killed. That's what's going to happen. And it's going to spook the guys in the woods. This is all going to come apart, badly."

"The crazy mother-fuckers . . . ?"

"The CMFMC. Jesus, didn't those jackasses at the DEA tell you anything?"

I figured out what the first three letters of the acronym were, and then I realized what the last two stood for. *Motorcycle Club.* Where had I seen those letters? Right. On a motorcycle jacket. With a knife stuck through them.

"No, no," I said. "Sorry. I thought it stood for something else."

"Something else? What else could it stand for?"

"'Callous,'" I said. "Maybe 'carefree.'"

He was quiet for a long time—long enough that I was starting to wonder if I had pushed him too far—and then he let go with another one of those monster exhalations. This guy telegraphed everything.

"You really are a fucking piece of work," he said.

"I get that on occasion," I said.

"When I first heard about you, I couldn't believe it. It was just too ridiculous. Rising porn star gets popped for cocaine trafficking. Goes to CCI where he shanks a guy in the shower who was trying to rape him. Jesus, that's some back story. Lady I talked to said it was the most insane deep cover story she'd ever seen."

I bit back a laugh that would have blown it for me. "Yeah, well, the best ones are the weird ones," I said. I didn't even know if that was true, but what the hell. So the missing decade of my life was now some deranged narrative for secret work as an undercover DEA agent? Like I was going to contradict the deputy.

More importantly, though, who had he been talking to? Who was this lady?

"So, the bikers are going to whack Boreal," I said, getting back to the problem at hand. "Why? Is he going to squeal?"

"He doesn't know enough to squeal to anyone, but they don't know that. They're paranoid, man. They want the weed. They want it all. And they know something isn't right."

"Boreal knows about you," I said.

He didn't say anything, which suggested that I had hit the mark on that one. But *what* Boreal knew, I didn't know. And then I made another intuitive jump. "You and the sister," I said. "Dorothea."

"Shit," he said softly.

And that's when I knew the reason he'd been sitting outside the restaurant yesterday, and why he had been looking at my car. He had been watching Dolly.

"How deep is she in this?" I asked.

"She's not," he said quickly. "She's really not."

"But her brother is." I took another guess. "And if her brother dies in County, she's going to blame you, isn't she? You said that you'd take care of him, didn't you?"

"We need to fix this," he said. The stress was creeping back into his voice.

"How are *we* going to fix this?" I asked. "You're the sheriff's deputy. I'm the deep cover guy. You think I'm going to go over to Santa Maria and flash some ID and tell them to let the kid go? And for what? You haven't given me anything yet. All I've got is a bunch of weed some fuck-up juvie graduate was trying to sell to stoners at what? Some state park or something?

"And you? You're trying to sell me on this idea that you're in some serious shit, but come on, what have you shown me so far? Oh sure, these CMFMC are badasses on bikes and they're into God knows what, but seriously? I can call any casting agency in Hollywood and get two dozen dudes to play those parts in an hour. If *crazy motherfucker* is all you got, then what am I going to tell the AG? 'Hey, here's a case. These guys are clearly up to no good. Let's arrest everyone.'"

He started to fidget. "Okay, okay," he said. "You need more. I get that. I can get you that."

"Let's get David out of jail first," I said. "How long after they arraign him until he goes to County?"

"Seventy-two hours," he said. "Give or take."

"And if he makes bail?"

"Bail? He's a punk who's been in and out of the system for his whole life—"

"I don't give a shit about his record. Can he make bail?"

He got it. "If he does, then he doesn't go to County."

"So let's start there. I can't help him if he's stuck in the system. You're the local with some pull. You need to make sure he gets out."

"How am I going to do that?"

"Well, the simplest way is fuck up the arrest report—"

"That's not going to fucking happen."

I raised my hands. "Okay, then you're going to have to find someone to post bail. His sister have any money?"

"No," he said. I could tell the idea was almost as distasteful as suggesting he falsify evidence. Good to know where he stood on currying favor with Dolly.

"How about bail bondsmen. You got any favors you can call in?"

He thought about that for a minute. "Yeah," he said. "I might."

"You do that. And then call Dol—Dorothea."

"Okay," he said. "And then what?"

And now he was asking me for advice. Those wheels in his head were grinding on a new problem now.

"Once the kid is out on his own recognizance, we need to convince the CMFMC there is nothing to worry about. Right?"

"Right."

"Is there anything to worry about?"

He hemmed and hawed for awhile.

"You and I are going to have to talk some more," I said. "But not now. You have things to do. And I . . ." I trailed off, not quite sure what I was going to do.

"What?" he asked.

I rattled the handcuff still attached to my wrist. "Can you take this off?"

"Oh, yeah, sorry." He came closer, and grabbed at my wrist. Up close, I could tell that his deodorant wasn't up for all this subterfuge.

"We, ah, we shouldn't be seen together," he said after he had taken off the handcuffs.

"That's fine with me," I said.

"You know how to get back to your car?" he asked.

I glanced around at the unlit warehouse and empty lot. "That way?" I pointed in a random direction.

He shook his head. "See that light over there?" he said, pointing in the other direction. "Turn left there. Go two blocks. Turn right. Three more blocks. Maybe four. And you'll come to the road that runs past Rye."

"You're going to leave me here?"

"We shouldn't be seen together," he repeated.

"How are you going to contact me?" I asked.

"I know where you're staying," he said.

So does everyone else in this town, I thought.

"I'll call you tomorrow," he said. "At the hotel."

He got into the SUV and turned on the engine. I stepped back from the car, and watched his taillights circle around, He stopped at the intersection he had pointed out, and as he was turning left, he finally turned on his headlights.

I looked up at the moon, which was hanging like a lopsided smile.

"Well," I said to no one in particular. "This got interesting."

CHAPTER 16

I was lost in a dream of fishing for marlin, and since I had never been on a boat nor done any fishing, the dream had been a cavalcade of physical comedy at my expense. I was saved further mental embarrassment by the ringing of a phone, which intruded in the seaspray-soaked dream like a celestial game show buzzer. God buzzing me out for being clueless about how to haul in a thrashing fish.

The sheets of the hotel room bed were twisted around me, standing in for both my inept handling of the fishing line and as the claustrophobic all-weather gear the fishing boat guide had insisted I wear. I shoved one of the overstuffed body pillows out of the way, and fumbled for the noisy phone on the nightstand.

"Hello?" I mumbled into the receiver as I dragged it close.

"Butchy Boy!" Mrs. Chow's voice sang in my ear. "You are doing well?"

"Mrs. Chow," I said, stifling a groan. "Why are you calling me?"

"You never returned my call."

I ran a hand over my face, wiping off a sheen of dream sweat. Salty, on the tongue. Like seawater. "When did you call me?" I asked. "Why—no, how did you find me?"

"I call the hotel. I ask for you. They connect me to your room. It's not complicated."

"Not when you put it like that," I said. I sat up, and looked around the hotel room. Remembering where I was and how I had gotten here. "What are you doing?"

"I'm calling you, Butchy Boy," she said. "What does it sound like I'm doing?"

"What time is it?"

"Nearly ten o'clock. Well past time for you to get out of bed."

"I'm not—" I started, and then gave up. I was still in bed, actually. I really wanted to hang up on her. She'd call back, assuredly, and maybe I'd actually be awake the next time.

"Are you in trouble?" she asked.

"No," I said. "Well . . ." I rephrased.

"I take Baby Baby down to the salon today to get his hair trimmed. Orchid. You know it, yes?"

"Yes, I know which salon that is." All of the salons were named after flowers. It made them more distinctive than *Chow Salon No. 4*, for example.

"Linn tells me she had a pedicure the other day. Tall, American woman. Business suit. Nice shoes. Had Compassionate Crimson Alacrity put on—"

"Mrs. Chow," I interrupted. "What does this have to do with why you're calling me?"

"Anyway, Linn tells me this woman, she makes a phone call during her pedicure. Talks to someone about someone else, like she had been digging up dirt on this person. No names, of course. But Linn, she hears this woman talk about naughty adult movies and prison terms. CCI, Butchy Boy. Tehachapi."

"Yeah, yeah. I know those names," I said.

"This woman gets all mysterious after that. Says things like 'I can neither confirm nor deny that statement.' Like in the movies. By this time, Linn—she is a nice girl, that one; she would make you a good girlfriend, Butchy Boy."

"I don't need a girlfriend, Mrs. Chow," I said, trying to ward off the conversational digression that was threatening.

"You do, Butchy Boy. You certainly do. A grown man like you needs a woman to take care of him. Linn—she was one of my girls who did your toes that time. In the house. You remember?"

"I do," I said. "And I'm not sure I've forgiven you for that yet."

"Never you mind that," she continued. "Linn is a good listener, and she hears this woman talk about secrets. Says things like 'too good to be true.' 'I can neither confirm nor deny that statement.' And then, when Linn is done, the woman pays her in cash—big tip too!—and tells Linn, 'I only lied a little, mostly about the beefcake. I hope he's having a good time, visiting old friends.' What does that mean, Butchy Boy? What is this beefcake?"

"It's a slang word," I said. "You know, cheap talk. It mean 'stud.'"

"What is 'stud'? Like a horse?"

"She was talking about me, Mrs. Chow."

"Aha! I knew she was. You are beefcake, then?"

I couldn't tell if she was serious or pulling my leg, and that was another digression that could wait. "Who was this woman?" I asked.

"Linn had never seen her before," Mrs. Chow admitted.

"So, let me see if I have this straight," I said, getting my brain to track all the pieces. "A woman neither you nor Linn recalls seeing before comes into the salon, gets her toes done, and while she's there, she calls someone and reports to that person salient data about an individual that sounds an awful lot like me. And then, before she leaves, she tells Linn what she's done, knowing full well that Linn is going tell you." I paused for a second. "How did you know where I was?"

"I didn't," she said. "I called many hotels."

"And before that? Who did you call?"

"I just called hotels," she protested. "Many, many hotels."

"Mrs. Chow, there are thousands of hotels in southern California. You didn't call all of them."

"I did. How else was I going to find you?"

"All because of a woman getting a pedicure."

"A professional woman," Mrs. Chow corrected me. "Employed by the federal government."

Pieces finally clicked into place. Hackman had mentioned a woman. Someone he had talked to about me.

"And that's all she said to Linn?" I asked, suddenly much more interested in why Mrs. Chow was calling.

She paused a second, and in the background, I heard Baby Baby barking. I prompted her again. "Mrs. Chow? Am I in danger?

"Are you?"

I rolled my eyes. "Mrs. Chow, you can't keep—" I caught sight of the time on the clock, hanging on the wall. "Shit," I said, changing mental course.

"What is it? Are you being held hostage? Can you tell me?"

"No, I'm not being held hostage," I said. "Look, Mrs. Chow, I have to go. Everything is fine. Thanks for checking in with me."

"But, but—" she started.

"Bye." I dropped the receiver on the phone base, missed the cradle, and the phone clattered off the base, bounced off the bedside table, and then hung down the front of the table. Mrs. Chow kept talking as I struggled to fully extricate myself from the bed.

Hack had been talking to the DEA about a deal. When I showed up, he had called in and asked about me. Someone had passed along the request—maybe it was some sort of inter-agency information sharing. Who knows. Regardless, the request had ended up with a woman who had gone out of her way to let Mrs. Chow know she had vetted the request, knowing that Mrs. Chow—like Linn—would reach out to me. While Mrs. Chow's tenacity was legendary, I didn't believe for a second she had called every hotel in southern California, which meant this woman had also hinted at where Mrs. Chow could find me.

Who was she? Did she work at the DA's office? FBI? DEA?

No, not DEA, I realized. She had put the idea of me being an undercover DEA agent in Hack's head with her 'I can neither confirm nor deny that statement' bullshit. He had run with it, because he had been waiting to hear from one.

Dolly's bother was supposed to be arraigned this morning. If Hack had squeezed a bail bondsman into covering David's bail, there was a chance Dolly's brother was going to get out today. I had to be there. And right now, I didn't even know where the courthouse in Santa Maria was.

This puzzle about who was setting me up as an undercover DEA agent would have to wait. But, in the meantime, I could use it to get David Boreal out of danger.

Provided I got to the courthouse in time.

Signs on the freeway directed me to the downtown area of Santa Maria, and I eventually found the courthouse. I parked my car and hustled my way into the line for the courthouse. The building was arranged like every other city courthouse, and I made my way up to the floor where arraignments were being held.

Outside the courtrooms, Dolly was sitting on a bench near the windows. When she spotted me, her eyes widened. She looked left and right, thinking about fleeing, and I sat down next to her before she could decide what to do.

"Is everything okay?" I asked.

"How did you know I was going to be here?" she asked. She wore little makeup, and her face was pale. Her eyes were red, and she looked like she hadn't slept much last night.

"I, uh, you weren't at the front desk," I said, quickly trying to figure out an explanation for my presence that wouldn't blow my . . . cover. "They, um, said you were taking some personal time, and I . . . I sorta guessed, based on what I heard you talking about last night. You know, in the restaurant. When your brother called."

It was weak, but she nodded as I lamely talked my way through an explanation.

"He was picked up last night," she said. "There were . . . there were drugs in his van."

"Oh my god," I said. "Were they his?"

She gave me a look that said I had just asked the dumbest question in the world, but I didn't take it personally. The look meant that she had bought my story.

Whatever the hell that was. Just an ex-con posing as a DEA agent with a back story of drugs and pornography, who was trying to help a pretty woman out with her drug-dealing brother, who, in turn, was caught up with a corrupt law enforcement officer and a bunch of crazy motorcycle riders, who were running drugs up and down the 101.

This was the sort of thing that Mr. Chow had warned me about. *Never do a selfless deed*, he had told me once when we had been lifting weights in the yard. *You expose your soft belly. You fall into that trap. But you're not a good person. You can't help anyone, and kindness will get you killed.* He was supposed to be spotting me, but when I got the bar and weight off the stand, he came around and punched me in the gut. I almost dropped the weights, but didn't, because part of me knew he was going to do something like that.

Protect yourself, was one of his annoying maxims. *Always.*

I did one rep, even as my stomach muscles cramped, and then I dropped the weights onto the metal brace with a loud clatter. *If you get on that bench, I will drop the bar on your neck*, I said to him.

I know, he said. *That's why I'm doing legs today.*

And looking at Dolly now as she covered her face and shook her head, I knew why I was exposing my soft belly. I wasn't in prison anymore. You can't remain in solitary confinement when there are no bars separating you from other people.

For all his talk, Mr. Chow had shown me kindness. In his own way.

"What are the charges?" I asked gently.

She dropped her hands, and stared up at the ceiling. "Possession of an illegal substance. Intent to sell an illegal substance. Trafficking an . . ."

"An illegal substance," I finished for her. "How much?"

"The back of his van was full."

"So they're not just stacking up bullshit charges because he cruising around with his windows rolled down and a joint shoved between his lips," I said.

"He did that already," she said. "When he was fourteen. On a golf cart."

"Really?"

She looked at me. "You're not impressed with that, are you?"

"A little bit," I admitted.

"Men," she sighed.

"They're everywhere," I said.

A ghost of a smile flittered across her lips.

"Do you have someone looking into bail?" I asked. "Is his juvie record still sealed?"

"Yeah," she said tiredly. "There's a bondsman in there"—she waved a hand at the nearest courtroom—"along with a PD and Frank—Deputy Hackman."

"Who?" I asked, pretending to not notice her slip.

"I know one of the sheriff's deputies," she said. "We went to school together, a long time ago." A haunted expression ghosted across her face. "We went to prom together, Franklin and I. We talked about getting married a lot. He did, at least. And moving to San Francisco."

"But that didn't happen."

"Nope," she said, shaking her head slowly.

"Family stuff?"

"Mine or his?" she asked in return, looking at me.

"Whichever," I said.

"It was my family," she said. "David and Mom. I was the adult between the three of us. Mom was starting to show signs of early onset dementia when David was in high school, which probably contributed to his . . . delinquencies. I was in school, down at UC

Santa Barbara, and when I graduated, I moved back in to take care of Mom. And David? Well, David was *David*. Still is."

She looked down the hall. She had shared her family secret with me, and now she couldn't look at me. I had to bring her back. I had to reciprocate in some way. Otherwise . . .

"My sister was killed by a drunk driver," I blurted out.

She stirred slightly, but that was all I was going to get.

"Who also happened to be my father," I continued.

I held my breath and waited. Slowly, she turned her head and looked at me again. "That's . . ."

"I know."

And now that I had started, I had to finish. I had to tell the whole story.

"We were watching TV. Mom, Cathy, and I. Some disaster movie, I think. It involved a boat. I was in the kitchen, making popcorn. We had one of those fancy hot air poppers, and it didn't work quite right. You had to stand there, and shake it every few seconds to make sure the kernels kept moving. I was in the kitchen, and I kept shaking the popper and then darting over to glance at the TV. I saw the headlights, but I was too busy trying to watch TV and make the popcorn. Usually, when he comes home, we see the lights when he turns into the driveway, you know? But this time, they didn't flash past. They turned and kept coming. I went back to shake the popper, and that's when his car came plowing through the picture window."

"Oh my god, Butch. That's . . . Did he . . . ?"

"Yeah," I said. "My dad drove the car right into the house. Killed my sister. Broke my mother's arm and hip. Dad had a busted lip and a gash on his forehead. I was the only one who wasn't injured. All I was doing was trying to make sure the popcorn popped evenly."

She stared at me, and then, in a rush, she leaned over and kissed me on the lips.

"What was that for?" I asked, when all the fireworks stopped going off in my head. My tongue tingled, like I had licked a battery, and all I could smell was the fresh scent of her shampoo.

"Because, I wanted to last night," she said shyly. "But I didn't, and all last night, when I was lying in bed—after getting home from the police station—all I could think about was kissing you."

"And now you have," I said.

"I have," she said. Her teeth worked at her lower lip. "I kind of want to do it again."

"Me too," I said, and I leaned toward her.

The courtroom door opened, and a familiar shape in a familiar uniform pushed his way out. He was holding his hat in his hand, and he stopped for a second when he spotted me next to Dolly.

"Ah, Ms. Boreal," Hack said, somewhat stiffly. "The arraignment is done."

He glared at me, and Dolly misinterpreted his look.

"Franklin—Deputy Franklin Hackman, I mean—this is Robert Bliss," she said. "He's a friend."

"Howdy," Hack said.

I replied the same, and even gave him a little wave.

"They got bail," Hack said. "Tortes is taking care of it. He'll have some paperwork for you to fill out, and, yeah, you'll just have to talk to him about it. Downstairs, in a bit, I think."

"Okay," Dolly said. "Thank you, Deputy Hackman. And what about David?"

"They'll release him later. Once everything is all taken care of. You can give him a ride home."

Dolly shook her head. "I'm still so furious with him," she said. "I mean, thank you, Deputy. I don't know what I would have done if you hadn't been able to find Mr. Tortes to help me out. It means so much to me that David isn't going to jail right now, but I can't—I just can't see him right now. He makes me so angry."

Hack fussed with his hat. "He needs a ride home, Ms. Boreal. He can't just walk out of here."

"Could you give him a ride?" she asked.

"I will," I said before Hack could reply. "I'll give him a ride."

Dolly turned toward me, her hands finding mine. "You will?" She didn't see the look of relief that swept across Hack's face.

"Sure," I said. "I'd be happy to."

"That's wonderful. Thank you." She squeezed my hands, and then looked at Hack, who waved his hat around for a second, and then ended up pointing toward the stairs at the end of the hall. "Oh, of course," she said. "I'll go take care of the paperwork."

She stood and then turned to me. "I suppose I should go back to the hotel," she said. "You'll stay with David until I get off work?"

"Absolutely," I said.

"Thank you," she said. She leaned over and kissed me lightly on the cheek. "I don't know where you came from, but I'm glad you're here."

She stood up, and went over and embraced Hack. She kissed him on the cheek before he could get over his surprise. "Thank you, Franklin," she said.

"No problem, Ms. Boreal," he said gruffly, fussing with both his hat and his belt. "Glad I could help."

She smiled, glanced at me once more, and then hurried off toward the stairs.

We watched her go, and when she had disappeared down the stairs, Hack jammed his hat on his head. "You stay clear of her," he hissed.

"It's been a long time since prom, Franklin," I said. "She's a big girl now. She can make her own decisions."

He got in my space, the brim of his hat nearly hitting me in the forehead. "You leave her out of this," he said. His face was red and shiny.

"Do you want my help or not?" I asked.

He chewed on that for a second. "Boreal will be cut loose within the hour," he said finally. "The public defender got lucky with the judge, but that doesn't clear Boreal. He's out on bail, but the charges are still pending. The sheriff's office is going to make something stick to him, and when it does, he's going to jail."

"I guess we'll have to take care of everything else before then," I said.

He poked me in the chest with a stiff finger. "He'll talk," he said. "He'll tell you where he got the weed, and he'll tell you about the CMFMC. You'll see. You'll see how big this thing is."

"Yeah," I said. "We'll see, won't we?"

CHAPTER 17

DAVID BOREAL WAS TROUBLE. HE SLOUCHED OUT OF THE COURT-house, wearing baggy pants, an oversized jacket, and a Dodgers cap pulled sideways across his head. His face was long and gaunt, and tufts of hair sprouted from his face like he couldn't quite muster up the attention span to grow a whole beard. He stopped his slow strut when I called his name, and he peered at me, blinking slowly like he was trying to match my face to a sluggish parade of mug shots in his brain.

"You don't know me," I said as I walked up to him. "But I'm your ride."

"Nah, man, I'm good," he said, waving a hand at me. "I got someone coming."

"Okay," I said. "I'll wait with you."

"You . . . you don't need to do that." He shuffled away from me.

The automatic doors to the courthouse opened, and a florid man in a leather jacket and boots came stomping out. He had a round face and a round head that was mostly bald. What hair he had left was long and stringy and pulled back in a weasel tail that lay limply down his back. "David!" Weasel Tail hurried over to us, his boots clicking against the pavement.

"Aw, man, what?" David pulled at his pants, which slipped back down as soon as he let go.

Weasel Tail looked me over. "You the boyfriend?" he asked.

"I guess I am," I said. Why not? I was already impersonating a DEA agent.

"I put up the bond for you, David," Weasel Tail said, which made him Hack's bondsman, Tortes. "If you don't show next week, they keep that money. And then your sister's going to owe me, okay?"

"Yeah, yeah, I know," David said.

"I should be locking you up in my basement," Tortes said. He looked at me again. "I must be out of my mind," he said. "This kid's a total flight risk."

"Where's he going to go?" I asked. "Dad's dead. Mom's gone nuts. Dolly is all he's got left, and she gave everything up to watch over him." I glared at David. "To make sure he didn't fuck up."

David opened his mouth to protest.

"And yet, here we are," I said.

He closed his mouth and stared at the pavement.

"He's not going to run," I told Tortes.

"Yeah? And who are you to make sure that doesn't happen?" he asked.

"I'm the guy who will find him, break his leg, and make him walk back. And if he whines, I'll break the other one."

Tortes stared at me, trying to decide if I was serious.

"What? You want me to snap a finger right now to show you I'm not fucking around? One of yours or one of his?"

He blinked several times as my questions sank in, and then his round face split into an open-mouthed laugh. "You are a funny man," he said, slapping me on the arm. "He's all yours. But I need him back here on Tuesday."

"He'll be here," I said.

Tortes waggled a finger at David. "Twenty-five K," he said. "That's what I'll be getting from your sister if you aren't here. Got it?"

His point made, Tortes waddled back to the courthouse, leaving me and the expensive pothead on the sidewalk.

"Twenty-five K," I said. "That's a lot of dime bags."

"It's nuthin'," David muttered.

"Must be nice to know how much you're worth to someone," I said. I pointed toward my car, parked across the street. "Come on, 25K. Let's go for a ride."

"Don't call me that," he said.

"Earn a different name, then, bitch," I said, bumping him with my shoulder.

Was I being hard on the kid? Probably. But he reminded me of myself, years ago. Too frightened and too proud to admit it. All caught up in his own business. Not able to see past the brim of his baseball cap. And because I knew that he had no clue what it meant to have someone give a shit about him.

"Put your seatbelt on," I told David when we got in the car.

He ignored me, staring out the window at the traffic moving past the courthouse.

"I could put you in the trunk," I said.

"You going to break my leg first?" he asked. There was some defiance in his voice.

I sighed and started the car. "I was kidding," I said.

"No, you weren't," he said. And then, quietly, but not so quiet that I couldn't hear him over the throb of the engine: "Asshole."

It was going to be like that, apparently.

He remained slumped in the seat, refusing to look in my direction, as I navigated out of the downtown core, but when I drove past the onramp to the highway, he sat up a little straighter. As we drove out of town, he started to fidget. "You missed the onramp," he whined.

"I didn't," I said. "We're taking the scenic route."

"Aw, man, really?"

"You got a pressing appointment this afternoon?" I asked.

"No, man, it's just . . . fuck, really? The scenic route?"

"We need to have a chat, you and I," I said.

"No, man, I don't want to chat. Oh, shit. Man. This is no good. Can you just—can you take me back?"

"You want to go stay in Tortes' basement?"

"No, man, I don't want to stay in that dude's basement. I just want to go home. I just want—Jesus, can we just go back to the highway?"

"Is there something you're worried about?" I asked.

"You're going to take me out into the woods and rape me, aren't you?"

I laughed out loud. "No, I'm not going to rape you."

"You're not?"

"Is that what you think I'm going to do? Because I called you 'bitch' back there?"

"Isn't that what it means? You're going to make me your . . . you know . . ."

"Where did you get that idea?"

"I—it's just—you know . . . it's what happens in prison." He plucked at his jacket. "I'm soft, man. Look at me. They're going to send me away for all that weed, aren't they? And some bad dude is going to . . . to . . ." He started to sniffle. "It's just weed, man. I don't deserve to get fucked in the ass for that."

"You're not going to get fucked in the ass," I said. "Not by me. Not by anyone in prison. If you even go to prison. Look, you're not there yet. Sure, the sheriff's office wants to put you away, but come on, how many times have they tried that with you? Two? Three?"

California laws about weed were ridiculously harsh, especially when you're caught with a carload of pre-filled baggies. His juvenile record was probably filled with offenses involving smaller amounts, and while he was younger than Dolly, he'd been past that age for awhile. He didn't strike me as the sort of criminal genius who managed to avoided incarceration for the better part of a decade, which meant he'd managed to wriggle out of trouble a few times already. Maybe done probation and a bunch of community service.

This time, though? He was going down unless he could cut a deal.

Enter Butch Bliss, ersatz *boyfriend* and *undercover DEA agent* who was going to make all that happen, right?

"Let's figure out a way to keep you out of prison, shall we?" I said.

He slithered around in the seat, angling his body toward the door so he could stare up at me from under the brim of his cap.

"Talk to me," I said. "We've got some time before we get back to Los Alamos. Tell me an interesting story. Maybe I can help."

He licked his lips, but didn't say anything.

I was going to have to prod him, but what did I know?

"The Crazies know you are dealing weed?" I asked.

He flinched, which was answer enough.

I nodded, like I had known that all along, and I stared out at the winding road for a bit while I waited for him to start talking. Hack was involved in the weed business in this area, as was David. But there was more to it than that, and Hack was starting to get nervous. It had to do with the CMFMC in some fashion, and the simplest scenario said the CMFMC were running coke up and down the coast—probably using The Rose, near Los Alamos, as their club house. They probably had a pretty solid setup, and were now looking to diversify into other drugs. However, Team Weed wasn't so keen to get absorbed by Team Coke.

So where did David Boreal—wastrel weed wizard and all-around asshat—fit in this scenario?

He worked at—what had Dolly said?—a Shell station in town. I thought about what I had seen during my ten-minute tourist drive through Los Alamos, and I dimly remembered seeing one of Shell's yellow signs. It had been a gas station-slash-garage, with a couple of bays for car service. Stack of tires on a rack beside the building. David was barely qualified to pump gas, but maybe he had some hidden talents with a wrench and an oil pan.

It reminded me of my job at Speedy's Car Wash. It had been a good setup. Lots of cars coming and going. Nobody notices a car wash. They're like dump trucks—part of the infrastructure no one notices in their neighborhood. A small-town garage off a major highway wouldn't attract too much attention with strange cars coming and going.

"What are you doing for them?" I asked.

"Nuthin," he said. "I don't do nuthin."

"So why all the fuss about the weed then?" I asked. "And where'd you get it? You growing your own? You got your own basement project?"

He shook his head at all my questions. Stonewalling me.

We were out in the country again, heading along the road that would eventually get us back to Los Alamos. The turnoff to Sisquoc was a few miles ahead. Nothing but vineyards and oil derricks. A dull drive if David was going to be all sulky.

I glanced in my rearview mirror as sunlight flashed off something behind us. David reacted to my change in posture, and he shot up in his seat. He twisted around, looking out the Mustang's back window. "What is it?" he whined.

"Nuthin," I said, aping his tone.

The road behind us curved less than a quarter mile back, and for a moment, that stretch of road was empty.

The road ahead of us was straight for another quarter mile or so, and I put my foot down on the accelerator, and the Mustang's engine throbbed in response. I glanced at the rearview again, and spotted three dots behind us. Too small for cars, and they were spread out across the road, instead of in a single-file line.

"Oh, fuck," David said.

Bikers. Crazy Mother-Fuckers.

CHAPTER 18

AT THE NEXT CURVE IN THE ROAD, I PUT MY FOOT DOWN HARD, and the Mustang—true to its name—leaped forward.

"It's them, isn't it?" David whimpered.

I spared him a glance. "Jesus Christ, put your seatbelt on, already," I snapped.

The Mustang rocked as a car sped past us in the other direction, and my gaze jerked back to the road. I was too close to the yellow line, and I corrected quickly. There was another curve coming up, and I had to slow down for it because David was still fussing with his seatbelt. As soon as we cleared the curve, I looked ahead for traffic, saw none, and slammed my foot down again.

"Do you know this road?" I asked David.

"Wha—what?"

"Do you know anything about this road," I said. "It runs all the way back to Los Alamos, and I know there's a turnoff for Sisquoc, which"—I glanced at the fields and the mountains beyond, trying to figure out where we were on the road—"shit, we may have already passed. And there's one that takes us up into the mountains and the highway up there. But what else, David? What other options do we have?"

He was still trying to get his seatbelt sorted out. The strap had auto-locked, which it did if you didn't pull it straight out.

I saw a sign for the turnoff that would lead us past Hidden Palms and all the way to the 166. I was pretty confident I could outrun the bikes on the open highway—either the 166 or the 101. The only trick was getting there without any trouble.

The dots were there in the rearview again, but bigger now.

Up ahead, the road opened up for the road into the mountains. The oncoming lane was empty, but as I started to turn the wheel,

I caught sight of a pair of bikes sitting on the shoulder a hundred yards or so past the turn. I jerked the wheel back, and David nearly slid into my lap.

"God damnit," I swore as I shoved him back into his seat. I lost control of the car for a second, and it wiggled down the middle of the road.

A truck, barreling right toward me, blasted its horn, and I got both hands back on the wheel in time to get the car out of his lane. My grip was tight on the wheel as I corrected again, keeping us on the road. David slammed up against the car door, and I heard his head bounce off the window.

I tried to split my attention between the road and David's seatbelt which was still loose in his hand. He looked dazed. Apparently his head wasn't so hard after all. I fished for the end of the seatbelt, caught it, and pulled the whole strap out as far as it would go.

The nose of the car drifted, and I corrected back into my lane, and with one more glance at the road ahead—making sure it was clear—I turned my attention to David's seatbelt. It wasn't easy to plug the passenger seatbelt in from the driver's side, but I managed it, and the strap slithered back across David as I let go.

As I leaned back into my seat, checking my environment, I caught sight of a black flash in my sideview mirror. A second later, a leather-clad shape on a loud motorcycle roared past us. Instinctively, my foot lifted off the gas so I wouldn't rear-end him.

I shouted something at the biker—even though he couldn't hear me. My twitch hadn't been much, but we had lost our momentum, The horses under the hood were going to have to work hard to make up for that loss.

And the biker knew I had faltered. He swerved back and forth in front of me, dropping back with each pass so that I had to either tap my brakes or risk hitting his bike. It was a ballsy move, and he thought he had my number. He would keep slowing down, forcing me to do the same, and within a few minutes, the other bikers would catch up.

I was in a '76 Ford Mustang. This was a car that proclaimed—very loudly—*I like 'em big and noisy.* It was a dick car, and sure, I drove it somewhat ironically, but I also drove it because a) it reminded me of the asshole I had been once upon a time, and b) it had a 5.0 L V8 engine in it and weighed somewhere close to three thousand pounds. The biker was playing that small predator wearing out its slow-moving prey with its quick, darting attacks game, but I was a goddamn grizzly bear, and I didn't have time for his shit.

The next time the biker swung across the lane, I mashed the gas pedal down and slammed the front end of the Mustang into the back of his bike. He tried to keep control of his bike, opening the throttle in an attempt to pull ahead of me, but I kept coming. I jerked the wheel to the left the next time I hit him, and it was like putting serious english on the cue ball on a pool table. His bike went down with a heavy crash. Sparks and bits of metal flew, and then the bike and its rider were behind us.

I looked back to check on the remaining bikers. The three who had been following us were getting close, and the second of the two who had been waiting for us on the turnoff was already behind me. He had one hand on the bike, and there was something in his other hand. Something hard and metallic.

"Get your head down," I shouted at David.

Something hit the back of the car, like a giant hand slapping us on the ass. A second later, a hole appeared in the back window and a big starburst of broken glass bloomed on the front windshield. Up high, closer to David's head than mine, but still too close for comfort.

"He's shooting at us," David moaned. He slouched lower than me. He had shaken off his momentary daze and lost his nominal whine somewhere in the process, which was a definite plus.

I reached up and thumbed the rearview mirror to get a better angle on the biker behind me, and nearly got my thumb shot off for my efforts. The car swerved as I flinched from the second starburst on the windshield.

As the biker steadied his bike behind us, I dogged the wheel to the left. When I jerked it back to the right, I slammed on the brakes. The back end of the Mustang slewed around, filling the road with the car, and the biker had to lay down his motorcycle or veer off the road. I gave him a second to commit, and then I let up on the brake, hauling on the wheel with both hands. We came out of the slide, and as we roared off, I glanced up at the rearview mirror, looking for the biker.

No sign. He had gone off the road.

Two down. Three to go.

I wondered if Clint and Brace were part of the trio behind us.

We had to get off this road. After the turnoff for Highway 166, there was nothing but the straight and scenic for a dozen miles. I could let the Mustang run, but the bikers wouldn't lose that much ground, and at the other end, there was nothing but Los Alamos and freeway interchanges.

I started looking for a turnoff, and when I spotted one on the left, I took it hard and tight, leaving a band of rubber on the road. The Mustang fishtailed as it left the pavement and hit the dirt road, and the wheels threw up a trail of dust and rock as the car got its footing on the road and took off again.

The access road was single-lane, and it twisted back and forth. I didn't bother looking back for the bikers. I was kicking up enough dirt they would have no trouble figuring out where I had gone.

So much for disappearing.

I didn't want to vanish so much as—

I didn't have a chance to finish the thought. As we came barreling around a curve, a chain link gate suddenly appeared across the road. I had a second to react, but that second went by really quick.

"Oh, shit!" David squealed as the Mustang sheared the chain holding the two halves of the gate together.

We roared out onto a wide plateau between a couple of low hillocks. In the center of the flat space was the hulk of an oil derrick, its massive head slowly rising and falling. A second chain link fence circled the base of the oil pumping machine, and as the car raced around the derrick, I looked for a second route off the plateau. And didn't see one.

Shit, indeed. There was no way off but the way we had come.

Swearing under my breath, I cranked the wheel of the Mustang, hauling the heavy car around the derrick. As we turned a half-circle and faced the way we had come, three bikes roared up from the access road. They split up immediately: two coming right at me, and the third circling around the far side of the derrick. I recognized Brace as one of the pair coming at us.

I gunned the car toward him, and he and the other biker started shooting. Bullets chewed up the hood of the Mustang and made more of a mess of the windshield. I hauled the wheel to the right, and the car turned to present the driver's side at the pair, who kept shooting at the bigger target coming at them.

I had put myself between David and the bullets. All very noble, but not the smartest move.

The bikes roared past us, and I cranked the wheel back, my arm muscles screaming. Something wasn't right under the hood of the car, and the back end felt sluggish. It was listing to one side, too, and when I pulled at the wheel, I realized the front left tire had been shot.

I aimed the car for the road down from the plateau and pressed my foot down on the gas so hard that my knee ached. "Hang on," I shouted at David. The car kept wobbling, and while we made it off the hilltop, I couldn't get the car to make the first turn. We careened up the side of the mound that ran along the road, crested it and then slid sideways down the other side. I got the nose of the car pointed in the right direction, and vainly pumped the brakes in a pointless effort to stop our headlong rush to the bottom of the ditch.

The car hit, and my seatbelt held me down while the steering wheel punched me in the face.

I heard a whistling noise, like air escaping from a balloon, and I realized it was the sound of a human voice. Then, everything went black.

CHAPTER 19

WHAT DO YOU DO WHEN YOU GET PUNCHED IN THE FACE?

The ghost of Mr. Chow sat on the hood of the car, which was not nose-down in a ditch. The Mustang was in a field of wildflowers—radiant yellow and orange as far as I could see. The only crimson in this Technicolor scene was all the blood on my shirt and the interior of the car.

You get up and punch back, I said, and while the words sounded utterly fine in my mind, they came out of my mouth like gibberish. There was something wrong with my jaw.

So punch back, Mr. Chow said. His face was all round and shiny in the warm sunlight. The cancer hadn't eaten him up yet. Or this was just the way my brain wanted to remember him.

My arms were heavy, and when I tried to move them, it felt like they were being held down by leather straps.

Flow like water across stones, Mr. Chow suggested.

Flow this, I said, getting one arm loose enough to give him a middle finger salute.

Your anger gives you motion, he said, *but remember it is just like water. So difficult to direct.*

I got my other arm free, and instead of listening to him talk about flowing like water, I leaned to my left and shoved my shoulder against the stiff door. It took three tries before the door popped open, and between the second and third shove, Mr. Chow said something important, but I was too busy falling out of the car to listen.

I was too busy waking up to pay attention to my subconscious.

I blinked several times, and each time my eyelids hurt a little less. I was lying on my back, rocks jammed against my spine. A heavy aroma of gas and scorched plastic filled the air, and a haze of greasy black smoke drifted overhead. My right leg was still in the car because my foot was caught under the dash. There was safety glass everywhere, and little of the front windshield was still in its frame. The left front tire was flat, and a thin ant trail of flame was licking along the edge of the hood.

I pushed myself up, and tried to see if David was still in the car. No sign, and the passenger side door was open too.

Motorcycle engines grumbled in the distance, and I struggled to get my foot out from the car. Nothing was broken; my foot was stuck between the clutch and the accelerator pedal. My lower back ached, and parts of my face were unresponsive. The front of my shirt and pants were covered with splotches of blood—some of it still damp.

I couldn't have been out for more than a few minutes. Where had David gone?

I yanked my foot free and, ignoring the ache in my back, I went up the slope of the ditch, using both hands and feet. At the top, I collapsed on my belly, and scanned the surrounding area for any sign of David or the bikers. There was nothing moving but the inflexible derrick—going up and down like nothing had happened. With a groan, I stood up, and looked farther afield.

A trio of small shapes buzzed along the distant ribbon of the road—heading south, toward Los Alamos. The bikes were too far away to tell if any of them were carrying two passengers.

Fire flared on the hood, and I started to limp away from the car until I remembered the stash of cash I had hidden in the trunk. There was a panel in the trunk. I hadn't put all of Matesson's five thousand dollars in the duffel bag. This was my secret reserve.

I patted my pockets for a second before remembering the keys were still in the ignition. I slid down the slope, bounced off the open door, and ducked my head into the car. The odor of gas and oil was stronger inside the car, and I wrestled with my key ring for a minute before giving up and fumbling for the trunk release lever instead.

The fire was hotter as I scrambled back up the slope. The trunk lid was unlatched, but it wouldn't budge until I banged on it with my fists. Everything was jumbled together inside the trunk, and I shoved the junk aside so that I could get to the hidden panel. It popped open, and I dug out the remaining bricks of cash. I threw them over the crest of the ditch, getting them as far away from the car as I could. I grabbed a light windbreaker I had forgotten was in the trunk, and was halfway over the top of the ditch when the fire hit the gas line.

The car exploded in a noisy whump, and a ball of hot air, smoke, and fire rolled over me. I tucked and rolled down the far side of the ditch. My ears rang, and it felt like the back of my head had been singed. I was still holding on to one of the bricks of cash, and I spotted several others nearby.

A plume of black smoke chugged into the sky from the other side of the mounded dirt. That was going to attract some attention. I had to get out of here; I had to find David.

The bikers had him. They hadn't stuck around to make sure I was dead, which meant they had grabbed the kid and ran. Every second I sat there, they were that much farther away.

David Boreal was still in trouble, and this time, it was all my fault.

By the time cars from the sheriff's office, the rural fire department, and the oil company who owned the derrick showed up, I was at least a half-mile away. I hadn't seen any sign of David, and I had struck out across the open terrain, using the hillocks and ravines to hide me from the road until I was far enough away that I wouldn't be immediately connected with the burning car.

I found a tiny creek in the one of the ravines. I didn't drink any of the water, but it was enough to clean up some of the blood and dirt. It felt like I had a good gash across my forehead, and my nose was tender but not broken. My chest looked like it had been beaten with a meat tenderizer, and it was already turning purple and yellow.

I wasn't the prettiest of hitchhikers, but instead of a bit of thigh, I flashed some green instead. It took three hundred bucks to convince an old man in a beaten-up Ford to let me ride in the back of his truck. He was heading to the grocery store in the strip mall just off the highway on the southern side of Los Alamos, and I peered over the edge of the truck as he turned onto the highway and headed past The Rose.

There were a handful of bikes parked in the lot, along with a few other cars, but there was no sign of movement around the building. The same was true for the hotel when I got a brief glimpse of it through the screen of trees that ran along the side of the highway.

The old man bumped his truck into the lot at the grocery store, and parked it in a spot close to the road. He got out, locked up the truck, and stood there a moment, looking up at the sun. "I might buy myself some extra beer today," he said to no one in particular, and he laughed to himself as he tottered toward the store.

It wasn't a bad idea, but I couldn't rest yet. During the drive, I had had lots of time to lie on my back, feeling every bump in the road like someone was pounding on my kidneys, and think about the mess I had gotten myself into.

On the one hand, I could just go to a used car lot and spend what was left of my expense fund on a beater that would get me back to LA. I could tell Matesson that I hadn't been able to find Gloria. Maybe she wasn't even at the Hidden Palms Spiritual Center. He should hire a real PI, if he was so eager to find her. Leave me out of it.

Or, I could find a phone and call Hack. Tell him that I lost the kid, and that I wasn't really a DEA agent, and good luck with extricating himself from the crazy situation he had gotten himself into. Odds were, though, he wouldn't take that news very well. And there was the issue with my car, on fire, out in the oil fields. There would be a lot of questions raised, and if I wasn't around, Hack could spin any bullshit story he wanted. It would get back to LA, where various agencies would see the obvious television appeal in busting an ex-con with a record for drug trafficking for doing it all over again in a sleepy little town in the middle of wine country. Not to mention preying on the heart of the despondent sister of the goofy brother who got in too deep and was summarily carted off and executed by this nefarious ex-con drug kingpin.

Or, I could keep pretending to be an undercover agent for the Drug Enforcement Agency . . .

I hauled myself out of the truck, and went into the store where I filled a basket with a handful of useful items that would instantly transform a disheveled wreck of a man into a passably invisible member of society. And a cheap tourist T-shirt too. Using the change I got from the young man in the express lane who gave me a serious side-eye as I checked out, I used the pay phone outside to call the hotel.

"Good afternoon, Los Alamos Motor Inn," a pleasant voice answered.

"Hey, it's me," I said.

"Hello. Oh, hi," Dolly said as she recognized my voice. "Is everything okay?"

"Not really," I said.

"David?"

I swallowed and ducked my head. "We need to talk about that," I said.

"What's happened?"

"Nothing. Maybe. Hopefully." I gave up trying to sell that lie. "Look, I need you to get your stuff and leave right now."

"Now?"

"There's a chance that you might be in danger," I said. "It's not safe there at the hotel. Just hang up—when we're done talking—just hang up and go."

"What's going on?"

"I'll explain in a bit. Just—Dolly, just do this, okay?"

"O—okay."

"I'm at the grocery store on the other side of town. Come find me there. I'll be waiting for you."

"Right now?"

"Right now."

"And David?"

"We'll talk about him when I see you."

"Is he—"

I shook my head and beat my fist lightly against the side of the pay phone. "I don't know, Dolly," I said. "But we've got to get you safe. Just—please, okay?"

"Okay, okay," she said. "I'm doing it."

"Good. I'll be here."

"I'll . . . I'll be there in a few minutes." The phone went dead in my hand. I hung up the receiver, and rested my head against it for a moment.

And then I went to find the bathroom. I had already frightened her with what I wasn't telling her. Might as well try to not make it worse when she saw me. And from there, I'd have to figure out how to protect Dolly, find her brother, and figure out some way to pull both of them out of this mess. Ostensibly by busting both the weed network and the cocaine-running CMFMC. Good thing I had the whole DEA thing going for me. Well, as long as no one bothered to ask too many leading questions.

It all boiled down to Mr. Chow's two-word aphorisms. *Get up. Punch back.*

CHAPTER 20

I DIDN'T ANSWER ANY OF DOLLY'S QUESTIONS AT FIRST. I JUST GAVE her terse directions out of town until we were on Cat Canyon, heading north, and only then did I relax.

"What's going on?" she asked.

She was driving with both hands on the wheel, hunched forward with her shoulders raised toward her ears. She was pale; she hadn't released one iota of tension since I had last seen her a few hours ago.

Her car was a older-model sedan, and something rattled in the engine as she drove. It didn't look like it would get anywhere near the hundred and twenty MPH the speedometer suggested it was capable of, and when the wheels hit a bump, the entire front end rocked long after the bump was gone. It wasn't a getaway car—not by any stretch of the imagination—but it was a generic grey color, and would be invisible in any parking lot. Just like every other no-name sedan on its third owner.

"Why aren't you telling me anything?" she asked. Her voice was whisper-quiet, like she had been shouting for hours the night before.

"There's nothing to tell," I said. "Nothing that isn't speculative."

"Where's David?"

"I don't know."

"What happened to him?"

"I don't know."

"Is he dead?"

"I don't know."

"What do you know?"

"That my primary objective right now is getting you safe."

Her eyelids fluttered a little, and she glanced at me briefly before returning her attention to the road ahead of us. "Thank you," she whispered.

"Don't thank me yet," I said. "I'm just making things up as I go."

Her purse lay on the console between us. "Is your phone in there?" I asked. When she nodded, I opened her purse and rummaged around. "Can I use it?"

"What for?" she asked.

"Give me a sec," I said. I found her flip phone, and dug out the flyer from Hidden Palms from my back pocket. I dialed the number listed on the brochure, and when someone answered, I asked to be transferred to Natalie's desk. The operator asked me to hold for a moment, and then Natalie came on the line.

"Hi, it's Robert Bliss," I said. "I came out and had the tour yesterday."

"Yes, Mr. Bliss," she said. "I recall our meeting."

"Look, I wasn't completely honest with you," I started.

"Imagine my surprise," she said somewhat archly.

"I wasn't asking for myself," I said, ignoring her tone. "I really was asking for a friend of mine." I glanced over at Dolly. "Look, this is all very sudden, but look, I liked what I saw, and I'm not sure I'm going to get another chance at this, but can you do me an enormous favor and intake my friend this afternoon?"

"I don't know about this, Mr. Bliss. It's highly unusual—"

"I'm driving up there right now. I've got her in the backseat. She's out of it right now, and I figure I've got about two hours before she comes down off this high, and whoo! I don't think I'll be able to keep her under control. Not by myself. I need some help, Natalie. I really do."

Dolly was staring at me like I had lost my mind. As Natalie hemmed and hawed about the irregularity of it, I put the phone to my chest and tried to reassure Dolly. "It's just for a day or two," I said. "You'll be fine. No one will look for you there. They've got good security."

Before Dolly could protest, I put the phone back to my ear. "—not something we normally do, but—"

"I'm happy to pay cash," I said quickly, interrupting her spiel. "I've got almost two grand on me. Will that help with the paperwork?"

"That will—well, Mr. Bliss, this is all terribly unusual . . ."

"Come on, Natalie. Are you trying to tell me I'm first client who has shown up suddenly with an out-of-sorts friend and a fistful of green?"

"It's not the way we do things at Hidden Palms."

"Not ever, or not normally?"

"Not . . . not normally," she admitted.

"Perfect," I said. "I'm a big fan of flexibility and circumspection."

"We do strive for both here at Hidden Palms," Natalie said, the hesitation disappearing from her voice. All professional, now that we were past the awkward part of the conversation.

"We'll be there within the hour," I said. I snapped the phone shut before Natalie could say anything else.

"What are you doing?" Dolly asked.

"Checking my dear heroin-addicted sister into rehab. I just love her so much and I had to drag her away from her evil drug-dealing friends and get her somewhere safe. Think you can play the part?"

"This isn't going to work."

"Well, you're not coming with me to find David," I said. "And with him in the wind, I don't want anyone thinking they should grab you so as to lure David back from wherever he's run off to."

Which was a total lie, but whatever. Just add it to the long list I was stacking up.

"Do you think David is—"

"I don't know," I interrupted. "I really don't know, but I'm going to find him, okay? I promise you that."

That wasn't a lie.

We ran into actual traffic—a line of cars coming and going as if there was some obstruction in the road a little farther ahead. I knew what it was, and kept my mouth shut as we queued past a rubber-necking opportunity with police lights and fire engines.

"Some sort of fire?" Dolly asked as we eased through the gauntlet.

"I guess so," I said. I slouched in my seat, keeping my face back from the window.

Not far from the road, a greasy smear of grey smoke drifted lazily into the sky.

"Is that your car?" Dolly asked.

"Was my car," I corrected her.

When she looked at my face, she was reading the bandage across my forehead in a different light. "What happened?" she asked.

"I missed a turn," I said.

She looked out at the smoke again. "You don't strike me as the sort who *misses a turn*," she said.

"There were extenuating circumstances."

"Such as?"

"Bullets," I said. "And some bikers."

"And my brother?"

"He was making a lot of noise too," I admitted.

"Is he up there?" she asked, nodding back at the lights and smoke.

"I don't think so," I said. "He wasn't in the car when I woke up. And I couldn't find his bo—him."

"He's still alive?"

"I hope so."

"You *hope* so?"

"Those bullets weren't coming out of nowhere," I said.

"Who?"

"Who do you think?" I asked.

"The bikers?"

"Yep." I rolled my tongue around my mouth for a second. "You know why they'd want to get all bang-bang with your brother?"

She shook her head disgustedly. "I can guess."

"Drugs?"

"Of course."

"Was he using?"

"No!" She calmed down after that outburst. "Not the hard stuff," she clarified. "He was—is; Christ, he'll *always* be—a pothead."

"So, he was part of the infrastructure that moved it, then."

She nodded. "I guess so. I guess . . . I just didn't want to see it."

"At the garage?"

Her face was tense, and she was fighting back the urge to cry. I put my hand on her arm, and we didn't say anything for a few miles.

There was a second gauntlet rubber-necking at emergency vehicles. In this case, there was just a tow truck and a pair of SBSO cars. I didn't see Hack among the uniforms who were supervising the tow truck guys as they pulled a mangled bike out of the ditch.

No ambulance, though. Either it had come and gone already, or the bike had been abandoned.

"Turn here," I said, pointing at the exit that would take us to Hidden Palms.

She slowed down and signaled—bless her heart. After the cars passed in the other direction, she turned and we headed up the hill, away from all the excitement.

I hoped it would all stay down in the valley, but I felt that was a naive hope.

We parked outside the gate, and Dolly leaned against the wall as I called in on the black phone. A pleasant voice acknowledged our arrival, and after I hung up the phone, I turned to Dolly, who was staring up at the darkening sky. "You ready to play *Dear Sister, Zonked on Heroin*?"

"'Zonked'?"

"It's a technical term."

"Can I be 'flying' instead?"

"It's better if you look like you're walking away from a terrible crash-landing in the middle of an ocean," I said.

"Walking away? Like, on water?"

"Well, okay. Maybe an unexplored jungle somewhere."

"Do we really need to do this?" she asked.

"I don't have a better idea, and if we can sell this to these folks, then you'll be safe for a few days. Think of it as a spa vacation."

"I've never been to a spa," she said. "Not like this."

"Well, my treat, then," I said.

"What if—what if you don't come back?"

"If I'm not back in less than forty-eight hours, just tell them everything. Get the police involved. Because . . ." I trailed off.

"Because you'll be dead?"

"Well, I hope not."

"Me too. Why can't I go with you?"

We had been over this in the car, and I knew she knew the reasons. She wasn't asking to have that discussion again. She just wanted me to reassure her that everything was going to be all right, because she would have no control over anything once I left. She was just going to have to sit and wait, and no one liked being left behind with their imagination running wild. "Because I need to know you're safe," I said. "Otherwise, what am I doing this for?"

She offered me a fleeting smile, and pushed away from the wall as the gate started to open. "Do I stagger a bit or just list to the side?" she asked as she started toward the open gate.

"Listing is good," I said.

"Do I need to drool?"

"Don't oversell it."

"Fun wrecker," she said as she leaned against the edge of the gate and rolled herself into the compound.

"This is the voice of experience talking," I said as I followed her.

"Is it now? Did you do terrible things to yourself as a young man?"

"Define 'terrible,'" I quibbled.

"Things you did that you won't tell me now," she said.

"In that case, the answer is 'absolutely,'" I said.

"Fun wrecker," she repeated as she—listing to the left, like a good heroin junkie—staggered down the drive toward the main house.

I walked with her, hovering close like I couldn't quite trust her to not rabbit at the first opportunity. I didn't list or stagger, and I carried the paper bag with the money bundles in my right hand.

The air was clear and clean, and the sky was the color of bruised eggplant. The sound of music and laughter drifted toward us from the amphitheater behind the house, and it was easy to imagine we were wandering into another world entirely.

A pair of men in white were waiting, and as soon as I spotted them, like glowing ghosts outlined by the yellow lights along the front of the house, I was worried that it was the Terror Twins. This was the only real flaw in my plan: that Wilson and/or the two knuckleheads who escorted me out last time had found out I had been back. But, when nothing untoward had happened during my interview the other day, I surmised Wilson was one of those administrators who was too busy sitting in his office, drinking scotch, to bother with the minutiae of day-to-day operations. And, as we got closer to the waiting pair, I let out a sigh of relief that my luck still held. I didn't recognize either of the orderlies who were waiting for us.

"Mr. Bliss?" one asked.

"That's right," I said.

"I believe you spoke to Ms. Davis about an intake fee?"

"I did." I glanced around. "Right here?"

He shrugged, like my concerns weren't his concerns. He was just following orders.

"Okay," I said. I opened the bag and held it up. He looked inside and nodded at what he saw. "Very good, sir," he said, taking the bag.

He glanced at Dolly. "If you'll come with us, miss," he said. His pal came down the steps and moved around behind us—creating a clear direction for Dolly to go. Addict herding.

Dolly looked at me, crossed her eyes slightly, and then collapsed in my arms. "I'm sorry, Butch," she sobbed on my shoulder. "I'll try to be good." Playing it up for the benefit of the orderlies.

"I know you will," I said. I squeezed her back, not in a rush to let go.

"And I'll find your friend," she whispered in my ear.

"That's—" I started, but I was interrupted by her lips covering mine. She hammed it up a bit, setting her teeth on my lower lip and tugging.

"I don't want to go," she pouted.

I extricated myself from her embrace, as the second orderly approached and lightly turned her toward the steps. She hung her head, looking back over her shoulder, as she shuffled up the steps and toward the door. I remained where I was and watched her go. Part of me was suddenly afraid that I wasn't going to see her again, but I shoved that fear back down into the darkness and smiled bravely.

After she and her new friend had gone inside the house, the remaining orderly indicated I should follow him. We went into the house too, and I looked for Dolly as we walked through the foyer, but she had already been spirited away behind one of the other doors. The orderly led me down the hall to the Consultations room, where he left me alone with the glaring picture of El Illustro. I poured myself a glass of water from the side table, and drank it greedily, wishing it was bourbon instead.

A few minutes later, Natalie entered the room with a folder and a clipboard in her arms. She was just as impeccably attired as yesterday, and seemed completely unruffled by my unexpected arrival late in the day. "Good evening, Mr. Bliss," she said, offering me her hand.

"Good evening, Natalie," I said.

"I see you've had some water," she said, indicating we should sit on the couch.

"Yes," I said. "I figured I might as well make myself at home." As soon as I said it, the turn of phrase struck me as slightly wrong, and I must have made a bit of a face because Natalie immediately tried to assuage my concerns.

"It's okay, Mr. Bliss. We'll take good care of . . ."

"My sister," I said.

"Your sister," she echoed. "Yes, we'll take care of her. She will come to love Hidden Palms during her stay with us. We have had many satisfied clients refer to us as the home they always dreamed of."

"Of course," I said. "And I'm sorry about all that nonsense the other day. I was just . . . nervous about all this. It's one thing to talk about it, you know? And another thing entirely to do it, but when I got back to LA, I went to see her—to try to talk to her about getting some treatment—and she was gone. Her roommate—oh, man, what a piece of work that girl is—said she had gone out with friends, but I could tell . . ." I trailed off, and did a passable impression of a worried brother who didn't quite know what to do with his hands. "I'm sorry," I said again. "You don't care about all this."

"I do, Mr. Bliss," Natalie said smoothly. "But there is some paperwork we need to fill out. And we need to discuss the full range of services that you'd like to engage for your sister."

"Oh, right, right," I said. I glanced toward the door. "Did you get my—what did he call it? My *intake fee*?"

"I did," she said.

"Is that enough?"

"Let's not worry about that right now," she said. She opened the folder and took out a stack of papers and put them on the clipboard. She offered me the clipboard, along with a pen. "Why don't you start on these," she said.

I lied more often than not on the paperwork, and I suspected Natalie could tell where I fudged the facts in a few places, but she was good at closing a deal, and she didn't say anything. Like last time, she walked me halfway back to the gate. I went on out and stood in the parking lot. As I watched the gate close, I tried to convince myself this was a good idea. This was the right course of action. And then the gate stopped running, and it was all done.

Dolly was safe.

I got into Dolly's car, adjusted the seat and the rearview mirror, and switched on the overhead light so that I could look at some of the paperwork Natalie had given me, kind of like a party gift. It was a dozen pages of legalese which she had brushed over earlier, and I took some time to study it now. As I did, I saw why Matesson had hired me in the first place, presuming that Gloria—or whoever had dropped her off at Hidden Palms—had signed similar paperwork.

The documents set up a designated responsible party. In Dolly's case, this was me, and Hidden Palms insisted all of its billing be done via electronic banking. They would have the right to bill automatically, and the only way it could be stopped was by the patient—who was not the designated responsible party. The patient had to voluntarily check themselves out of Hidden Palms for the account to be closed.

And if the Center prevented you from access to the patient, then how would they ever know who was paying the bill? And how much it was?

No wonder Matesson wanted me to get Gloria out of that place. He couldn't tell his bank to stop paying Hidden Palms. The contract clearly said they had every right to bill until such time they were no longer treating a patient entrusted to their care. If he got lawyers involved, they'd probably respond in kind, and maybe even accidentally tell one of the gossip columnists at the *LA Times*.

It was a pretty clever setup. The only problem was I had given them a bogus checking account and bank routing number. When they tried to use it in the morning, they'd figure it out. The cash deposit I had given them might give me a day or two of leeway, but beyond that, they'd likely shove Dolly out the front gate.

I put all the paperwork aside, and started the car. The engine sputtered and nearly died on me before catching. It coughed and wheezed, sounding more and more like an experiment thrown together at the last minute for a school science fair. "Come on, you old nag," I muttered, patting the dash.

That's what the hero always did in the western, right? Outnumbered and outgunned, he got back on his horse—and it was usually a decrepit animal that just wanted to hang out in the pasture and eat grass. He rode that horse back into town and faced the bad guys.

What about that Spanish fellow who had gone riding around the European countryside, all delusional about giants? He had a crap suit of armor and a broken lance and the giants were nothing more than windmills, but he was, like, perpetually stoned or something—some kind of metaphor, probably. What was his name? Sancho? No, that was his sidekick. Quixote. That was it. Don Quixote.

My high school English teacher had assigned that book, and I had hated it. Thought the guy was the biggest loser. All worked up about a woman who never even knew who he was (and certainly not the lady he imagined her to be). Tilting at windmills. I never understood why we had to read the book. Well, that was true about most of the books we had been assigned, but reading *Don Quixote* had been such a pain in the ass.

But, as I switched on the headlights and drove out of the parking lot, I thought I might track down a copy of the book when this was all over. I would probably still hate it, but maybe not.

Maybe the dude wasn't as fucked up in the head as I had thought back then.

CHAPTER 21

I GOT HER CELLPHONE OUT OF HER PURSE, AND TRIED TO FIGURE it out as I drove down the hill. It had a rudimentary contact list, but none of the names meant much to me. There was a call log too—time stamps were attached to the calls. I scrolled back and found the call she had gotten from David while we had been at dinner. There were two calls the following morning from a different number, and if I had to guess, that number belonged to Deputy Hackman.

I didn't want to talk to Hack—not yet—but it was good to know that I had a way to contact him, should I need it. I still didn't know enough about who the players were to piece much of the puzzle together. David was key, but so was Hack.

I doubted David knew much about the larger operations—not as much as Hack had led me to believe—but there wasn't much doubt in my mind that the bikers had nabbed him from the car after we had crashed in the ditch. The fact that they hadn't killed him (or me, for that matter) suggested they were still trying to get a handle on what was going on. How much damage control did they need to do? Who were all the players and what did they want? As long as these questions remained unanswered, I had time yet. I could still find David.

But where had they taken him? I gave that question all kinds of thought, but when I reached the 101 interchange, I didn't have a good answer. I didn't even have a good idea.

The winery tasting room was still open, and so I swung Dolly's car into the lot and parked facing The Rose. There were more than a dozen bikes parked in the lot beside the bar, and a half-dozen other cars as well. A couple of guys loitered near the front door, smoking and keeping watch. They didn't look over-agitated or nervous. Just another dull night watching the light die in the sky . . .

I sat in the car for awhile, listening to the engine tick. Drumming my fingers on the steering wheel. Where was I going to look for David? The service station? If they were moving drugs through there, why would they take David there? It didn't make much sense.

The hotel? Something nagged at me about the hotel, but I couldn't make the feeling manifest into a coherent thought. I knew Dolly wasn't involved—well, I really hoped she wasn't involved. It didn't make sense if she was—all of the drama about her brother would be play-acting, and for who? Hack? He liked her a lot more than she did him, and if she *was* involved, he would have to know.

Unless he was the real stooge here, but that was paranoid prison logic—the sort of thing that made total sense when you had no contact with the outside world. Most of the time, events and occurrences happened for rather simple reasons. A drawn-out, complicated conspiracy intended to massively fuck with one or two people was—more often than not—drama invented by someone with way too much time on their hands.

So, Dolly was out, and I was just tweaking about the hotel because Clint and Brace had jumped me there. They didn't have any connection with the hotel.

Or did they?

The nagging sensation wasn't going away.

It was the sort of problem your subconscious would figure out if you just left it alone for a little while.

Fortunately, I had some time . . .

What about Rye? The cook whistling on that reefer had clammed up when I had asked about the delivery van. And then, a few minutes later, Hack had shown up. Like he had known I would be there. And why would he?

My brain put it together. Because the cook had called him. Because I had talked about weed and then asked about the truck. In a rather ham-handed way. Like the way a not-so-bright undercover guy might try to ingratiate himself into a situation.

I had been thinking about talking my way onto the delivery van as a way to get into Hidden Palms, but someone was already using the van for nefarious purposes.

"Shit," I sighed. "That's how the weed gets delivered, isn't it?"

But where was it coming from?

Across the street, the door to The Rose opened, and a pair of bikers came out. They stopped to talk with the smoking squad, and in the neon light of the bar, I could tell one of the new guys was Clint. He was talking animatedly with the others. Delivering instructions, but there was some confusion and pushback about those instructions.

The little chat group broke up: the one guy went back into the bar, and Clint went to the lot where he climbed onto his bike. He pulled out of the lot, heading north, and I gave him a little head start before following.

I guessed it was time to find out what was north of town.

Light industrial warehousing and trailer parks, as it turned out. I hung back from Clint and nearly lost him when he turned off into one of the older trailer parks. There was nothing but darkness beyond the small cluster of mobile homes—farmland and scrub.

I turned off the headlights, and eased the car past the trailer park. There was an access road ahead, and I turned onto it. The road abruptly ended at a metal gate. The gate was attached to a fence that was a combination of iron rods and barbed wire, and it looked like it had been there for a long time. Beyond the fence was nothing but empty pasture. I left the car and jogged back to the trailer park.

Most of the trailers wore their age badly—quite a few had carports with leaning roofs and cars in various states of semi-abandonment. There were lights on in about one in four of the mobile homes, and at least half of the dark ones had wind chimes on their tiny porches. At the back of the park, where the road looped around and headed back toward the front, I spotted a couple of bikes parked out front of a dilapidated double-wide, along with a dusty Jeep 4 x 4.

I took a moment to make sure no one was watching me skulk through the neighborhood, and then I darted around the trailer next door. There was a kid's playset in back, and the swing creaked slightly as I passed, stirred by a slight breeze wafting across the dark field on my right.

In the corner of the lot was a plastic toolshed, one of those prefab types that you snapped together and put enough bricks along the bottom to keep it from tipping over in a stiff wind. It wasn't locked, and I eased the door open and cautiously peered inside. When nothing collapsed on me, I felt around and found a couple of long wooden handles—two rakes, something that jingled, and a shovel. I liked the shovel but it was too long, and so I kept feeling around. I found another shovel, but smaller. Not a kid's tool, but one for turning over dirt in the garden or something—a one-handed sort of something, if necessary. That would work.

I closed up the shed, and hopped the wooden fence that was mainly for show. Curtains covered the windows in the trailer next door, and lights were shining in two of the rooms. I crept closer, and was surprised by a security light that clicked on as I was halfway across the open space between the two trailers. I leaped forward, and somewhat breathlessly fetched up next to the trailer.

My heart thudded loudly, and it was almost impossible to hear anything other than my own panic. I tried to get my heart rate under control as I inched along the house. I peeked up at the corner of window where the curtain was slightly askew, and I could see a tiny slice of the room inside.

A man lay across a couch. His leg was in a white brace, and there were bandages up and down his arm. His head was wrapped with a bandage too, and what I could see of his face was covered in bruises. Judging from his medically provided attire, this was one of the guys who dropped his bike on the road.

I edged a little more to my right, and my breath caught in my throat as I saw a familiar pair of high-top sneakers. David was sitting in a overstuffed recliner, and broad strips of duct tape were wrapped around his chest and legs. Holding him in place. His head was down, and I couldn't tell if he was breathing. There was blood on his shirt, and it looked like he had bled on the recliner too. Not good.

Someone walked past the window, and I flinched away. Holding my breath, I did a slow twenty count before peeking up again. The curtain had moved some, and I could see more of the room. The kitchen was off to my right, and the guy stretched out on the couch was talking to someone. The guy pacing back and forth was Clint, and he didn't look happy.

"Goddamn it, Russo," he snapped, interrupting Couch Dude. Unhappy people talk loudly, which made it easier to listen in on their conversation. "I wanted you to talk to him. Find out what's going on, and now this—" He angrily indicated the still form in the recliner.

"Hey, man," Russo whined, raising his hands in protest. "It's not my fault. They wrecked my bike. I can barely walk."

Clint shook his head. "Did you hit him?" he asked the person in the kitchen.

I heard a dull sound, like a barrel rolling over. *Brace*, I thought.

"Once?" Clint raised an eyebrow. "Just once?"

Brace said something, but I couldn't tell if he was agreeing or offering a different count.

"What a fuck-up." Clint wandered over to the recliner. His body blocked my view, but it looked like he was checking on David. After a moment, he wiped his hand on the arm of the recliner and shook his head. "Get rid of him," he said. "I don't want to know."

"What about—" Russo started.

"Shut the fuck up and do what I tell you," Clint said. "And then put your ass back on that couch and don't fucking move until someone comes and tells you otherwise. I don't give a shit if it takes a week. You stay here, and let this all blow over."

"But my bike," Russo whined.

Clint stepped over the couch, and slapped Russo's brace. Russo yelped in pain, and Clint whirled toward the kitchen as Brace stepped into the living room. "Don't," Clint said. "Just don't."

Brace stopped. Clint had some balls. Brace's face looked like a black squall bearing down, and I sure as hell didn't want to be standing in front of that storm when it broke. I looked away, and my gaze fell on Russo. His face was all twisted up too, but from pain, and after a minute, I figured out the source of Brace's anger. He and Russo were family.

"I'm going back to The Rose," Clint said. "Going to talk to Doc and McCready. We need to find this asshole, and quick. Our friend with the hat is starting to come unglued. This is going to get messy really fast if we don't deal with it. You two"—he pointed at Brace and Russo in turn—"all you two have to do is dump this kid somewhere. And do it before morning." He stomped toward the door.

I dropped to the ground, and pressed myself up against the sheet metal skirt that ran around the base of the mobile home. I had the shovel underneath me, and I kept my head down as the door opened and Clint's boots clattered against the wooden landing. He came down the stairs in a rush, and his boots crunched across the gravel. He got on his bike, fired it up with a noisy rumble, and the sound of his bike echoed back and forth between the houses as he roared toward the street.

I stayed put until the echoes were gone, and then I carefully edged back up to the window again. Russo was still lying on the couch, and I didn't see Brace. I shifted around, trying to get a better angle, and the metal edge of the shovel scraped against the metal siding of the mobile home.

I snatched the shovel away from the siding, and ducked down again. I put my back against the mobile home and held my breath. Waiting to see if anyone had heard the noise.

The front door of the mobile home opened, and Brace stepped out onto the landing. He looked around slowly. Left. Right. Left again. And then he lowered his gaze and stopped.

He was looking right at me, and I wasn't that invisible.

Less than two ways to play this . . . was the thought running through my head.

"Hey," I said. "Nice night, right?"

And then I pushed off from the house and sprinted toward the fenced-in yard next door.

Heavy boots pounded the gravel behind me. Brace was coming.

CHAPTER 22

I CLEARED THE FENCE LIKE A PROFESSIONAL HURDLER, CUT AROUND the edge of the neighboring house, and pivoted back. When Brace came charging around the corner, I swung the flat side of the shovel at his face. He was quicker than I anticipated, and I caught him on the shoulder instead. The blow was hard enough to spin him around and knock him off balance. I dropped the shovel, and barreled into him.

We stumbled back, arms flailing, and he smacked into the car parked in the driveway. I fetched up next to him, my shoulder snapping the hood ornament off, and the metal spur tore my shirt. The car bounced on its shocks as Brace pushed off, and I rolled toward the other side of the car. His fist made a dent in the hood behind me, and I spun off the light assembly at the corner of the car before he could try to hit me again.

He roared like a bull moose and charged. I was half-turned when he slammed into me, and I got sandwiched between him and the car. When I went limp—easy to do when all the air has been forced out of your body—he slammed me against the car a second time.

Now I was seeing funny spots.

He reared back like he was going to headbutt me, and I managed to pull an arm free and chop the edge of my hand across his throat. He made a funny retching noise, and I flowed through a tai chi technique—Golden Rooster Stands on One Leg—and shoved the heel of my other hand up under his chin. His teeth made a hard click.

I drove my knee into his stomach, and when he doubled over, I flowed through Wave Hands in the Clouds, pivoting around him. It was my turn to slam him into the car, but I missed the window.

Brace's head bounced off the hard frame between the front and backseat. I aimed better the second time, but he was already rubbery enough that he just bounced off. When I let go, he collapsed.

He was still breathing, and his eyes stared blankly up at the night sky. *Good enough,* I thought, as I retrieved the shovel and headed back to the mobile home.

Russo was still on the couch, but he was sitting up and he had a sawed-off shotgun in his hands.

We both froze for a second, and the only reason the next second wasn't my last was because I was full of adrenaline and he was full of pain-killers.

He pulled the trigger on the shotgun and it made a terrible noise. I had already dropped to the floor and was scrambling toward him. I couldn't hear a fucking thing, and the air was thick with the smell of black powder. I lunged forward, leading with the shovel, and I felt it connect with something hard. I kept moving my arms, and when the second barrel went off, all the shot made a mess of the light fixture in the ceiling.

I dropped the shovel, jumped up on the couch, and started punching Russo in the face. The couch was soft, and it was like punching a pillow on a waterbed. I wrestled the now-empty shotgun from him and smacked him in the head with it. That seemed to do the trick.

I collapsed on the cushion next to Russo's limp body, and slowly slid off until my ass was on the floor. My heart was pounding in my chest, and my lungs were heaving like they were trying to inflate a hot air balloon. My ears were ringing, and there was something wet oozing down the side of my head and my neck. Other than all that, I was what Mr. Chow could call "pleasantly exerted."

The shakes started when I looked at the shot pattern on the back of the closed door and on the ceiling. Either one of those shotgun blasts could have pulped important parts of me. I had been lucky. Really lucky.

"No time to celebrate, Bliss." I thought I said the words out loud, but I only heard them as an echo inside my head.

The room was darker without the overhead light, and the only illumination came from the kitchen. I glanced at Russo, who really did look like a sack of beef tossed out the window of a fast-moving car, and then moved on to David, who looked, well, dead.

"Shit."

So much for saving Dolly's brother. I had fucked this up. I had gotten him involved and—

I stopped that line of thought. Yes, things had gotten out of hand, but was I truly responsible? David had been selling weed before I showed up. He still would have been popped by a sheriff's deputy—if not last night, then some night soon. They still would have arraigned him. And he still would have gone to county lockup, where the CMFMC would have shanked him.

Was that true, though? I paused and gave that some thought. Hack had told me that the CMFMC wanted David dead, but was that good intel? Standing in this rather bloody and awkward situation, I had to wonder about that assessment. Clint had been pissed at Russo and Brace for fucking things up here, as if the death of David *hadn't* been part of their plan.

But Hack had been so sure. Was that his own paranoia? Did he really have any idea what the CMFMC were up to? Or had he wanted something like that to happen? Something that would take David out of the picture.

But why?

I couldn't sit around and think it through. Brace was outside. He was going to get up sooner or later. I had to clear out before he came back. But I didn't want to leave empty-handed. There had to be something useful here. Something that I could use as leverage. I cast about the room one last time, and then headed into the kitchen to scope it out.

Nothing but cheap kitchen appliances and a sink overflowing with dirty dishes. I put the shotgun on the counter, and rifled through drawers. I found one of the bricks of cash Brace and Clint had taken from me, and I shoved it into my back pocket. In that same drawer was a box of shotgun shells.

I stared at the box, weighing the consequences of taking it.

The shotgun would be handy if the CMFMC came after me. But it was a close-quarters weapon, and I didn't want to be *that* close to any of these assholes again. This situation was all fucked up, and there wasn't anything more I could do to fix it. It wasn't my fight, and I had to get out before anyone else got hurt. Before Dolly got hurt . . .

Shaking my head at the stupidity of it all, I grabbed a dish towel and wiped down the stock of the shotgun, and then went and did the same with the shovel.

I was looking around the room, trying to figure out where else I might have left a fingerprint for a clever crime scene technician to lift when I realized David's eyes were open.

But he wasn't looking at me. He was looking over my shoulder.

I felt a cold breeze on the back of my neck.

CHAPTER 23

BRACE'S FACE WAS A MESS, THOUGH THE LOOK IN HIS EYE WAS CLEAR enough. Pure murder. He body-slammed me, and I face-planted into Russo on the couch. Brace went to work on my kidneys—left, right, left—as I tried to get away from him. Russo flopped beneath me, and I twisted around enough to take a wild backhanded swing at Brace with the shovel.

Brace stepped back, and that put enough space between us for me to catch my breath. He stood in the middle of the room, his fists raised.

I slid off the couch until my knees hit the carpet, and when he came at me, I banged the shovel off his shin. He backed off, and I struggled to my feet. His lips and chin were covered in blood, and when he grinned at me, it didn't improve his looks in the slightest. There wasn't going to be any discussion about setting aside our differences. In his mind, there was only one way this was going to end.

We circled until I was closer to the partially open front door. Behind Brace, I spotted the shotgun on the kitchen counter. And next to it was the box of shells. He hadn't seen it yet, but if we continued our slow dance around the room, he would.

And that would change things.

He was unwilling to come any closer as long as I had the shovel. He had felt it enough to be wary. But I had to get him to come at me. I made to stab at him with the shovel, and he flinched back. He flinched again when I threw the shovel, but there was no effort behind my throw.

I was already turning and heading for the door. I had exposed my back to him. I knew he would like that target.

But instead of running outside, I grabbed the doorknob and yanked the door open as I spun around and backed up against the wall. As soon as my back hit the wall, I shoved off. Brace had pulled up just short of the door, but when I bounced off the wall, it slammed into him.

He staggered back, and it was my turn to knock him into the couch. On top of his unconscious brother, who was going to be nothing but a huge bruise when he woke up.

I made a break for the kitchen.

I made it to the shotgun, but before I could any of the shells out of the box, Brace was in the kitchen too. He had picked up the shovel, and he nearly took my head off with a murderous swing. My fingers fumbled for the box, but all I did was knock it across the counter. A couple of shells tumbled out, and I grabbed at one of them.

Brace brought the shovel down in a vicious strike at my head, and I had no choice but to use the shotgun to block his swing. He hooked the edge of the shovel's blade on the barrel of the shotgun, and tried to pull the weapon out of my hand. Shaking me back and forth like a dog with a stick. He threw me to one side, slamming me into the counter and then back the other way. My grip slipped on the shotgun, and he yanked it out of my hands. The gun clattered on the linoleum, and he kicked it away from my end of the kitchen.

I had my back to the sink. I was surrounded by counters. There was a window behind me, but it was covered with a curtain. Brace stood between me and the rest of the mobile home. I was trapped.

"I'm gonna hurth you," he lisped.

"What? Hurth?" I said. "Oh, you mean, hurt." I pointed at his bloody face. "Did you bite your tongue off or something?" While my left hand was gesturing, my right was cautiously exploring the sink behind me. Looking for something useful. Something sharp. Or something I could make sharp.

Prison was good for learning how to make things sharp.

"Fuck you," he rasped.

My hand closed around a utensil.

He raised the shovel and came at me. I darted forward to meet him, getting inside his reach. I got my left arm under his right before he managed to hit me with the shovel, and then I stabbed at his face with whatever utensil I had found in the sink.

It was a fork, and I missed his eye with the first attempt, but you never stab once when you're using a homemade weapon, and I got him with the second try.

He howled and dropped the shovel. I lost a precious second trying to figure out how to get past him. With a deep growl, he went for my throat with his bare hands. Old school. No special tools but the ones we were born with.

I tried to break his grip, but he was a big man, and a very angry one. His fingers were tight about my throat. My heart hammered in my chest. My lungs were panicking. All I wanted was to get one more breath of sweet, sweet air, but I couldn't. Not with his bear paws around my neck. I flailed at his hands, but I couldn't get any purchase. Trying to grab his wrist was like trying to pull a tree out of the ground with one hand.

He shoved me against the sink. His face stretched into a hideous, bloody grin as he leaned closer, his one eye bright with the desire to watch me die. The fork was still sticking out of his other eye, and with all of my remaining strength, I slammed the palm of my hand against the end of the fork, shoving it farther into his head.

He stumbled, his weight heavy against my chest, and his grip around my throat loosened. His expression went soft, and I could pry his hands off. I shoved him away, and he bounced around the kitchen like a pinball ricocheting off bumpers, and then collapsed on the floor.

I took a few moments to reacquaint myself with air. It was glorious, and my lungs thanked me. My heart thanked me. And my brain was really thrilled to not have a fork stuck in it.

All checkmarks in the 'win' column.

I staggered past Brace, who was not going to get up again, and went to check on David, who was alive and freaking out.

A pair of police vehicles, their bubble lights painting the night red and blue, blew past me as I drove sedately away from the trailer park. I kept driving, minding my own business, and only after a second pair went screaming past did I dig out Dolly's phone and find Hack's number.

He answered on the second ring. "Dolly," he shouted over the sound of sirens. "Are you okay?"

"It's me," I said.

He didn't say anything for a minute, and I heard his sirens cut out. "Where are you?" he asked. "Where's Dolly?"

"She's safe," I said. "I'm going to get her now."

"There's a lot of chatter about gunfire and bodies at a trailer park," he said. "You know anything about that?"

"You should ask David Boreal," I said.

"He's alive?"

I didn't answer that question.

"We found your car," he said. "Once they put out the fire, they figured there had been a gun fight."

"They figured right."

"CMFMC?"

"What do you think?"

My throat hurt. I really didn't want any more of this mess. I just wanted to make sure Dolly was safe, and go back to LA. Matesson could get someone else to deal with getting Gloria out of Hidden Palms. "Your people are going to protect David now," I said. "There's enough evidence to get them to start looking at the CMFMC. You just have to get clear of it, and it will all take care of itself."

"And Dolly?"

"She's at the Hidden Palms Spiritual Center," I said. "I'm going to get her now. We'll go somewhere for a few days and then check in with you. Just to make sure everything is all wrapped up before she comes back."

He started to say something, but I heard his radio squawk in the background. "This is Lt. McCready, requesting emergency services at 3245 N. Poplar Road. I need some EMTs out here now!"

My lungs seized again, and my heart revved up—panic echoing in my ears.

McCready.

As he was leaving the mobile home, Clint had said he was going to talk to Doc and McCready.

Hack wasn't the only one at the sheriff's office working with the bikers.

I snapped the phone shut, and tossed it aside. My foot slammed down on the gas, and Dolly's car wheezed as it tried to live up to my demand.

David wasn't safe, and I had just told Hack where Dolly was.

CHAPTER 24

I SWITCHED OFF THE HEADLIGHTS AS SOON AS I TURNED ONTO THE dirt road that led to Hidden Palms, and when I reached the open meadow in front of the Center, I pulled the car over to the side of the road. I shut off the engine, pocketed the keys, and sat there for a minute. My ears still rang, but the noise wasn't as bad as it had been an hour ago.

I grabbed the damp towel I had taken from the mobile home. I opened the car door, and remembered at the last second that the dome light was going to come on. I squeezed my eyes shut as I jumped out of the car and shut the door quickly.

My night vision was pretty good for having driven the last mile or so in the dark, and I didn't see any movement. I stood still, listening, but there was no sound except for the gentle sighing of the wind in the trees, and somewhere far off, a bird screamed. It was answered by another bird even farther away. And that was it. Life in the wilderness.

Hugging the edge of the meadow, I worked my way along the tree line until I reached the wall surrounding the Hidden Palms Spiritual Center. I turned away from the gate and followed the wall until I reached the corner. The forest was close to the wall here, and I slipped under the shelter of pine and cottonwoods as I followed the wall. After a hundred steps or so, I stopped and gauged the height of the wall.

It wasn't more than eight feet tall, and holding the rolled-up towel in my hands, I did a standing jump and hooked my hands on the top. I pulled myself up, ignoring the complaints from my arms about the exercise, and peered over the wall.

There were two strands of razor wire running along the top.

Which was why I had brought the towel.

I dropped back down, reshaped the towel bundle, and tried again. This time, I got the thick wad of towel over the razor wire. My arms still bitched, but I did the pull-up, and managed to get my elbow onto the towel. Then I threw a foot up, and a leg, and the rest of me. The towel wasn't quite long enough, and a barb of the razor wire caught the cuff of my jeans. Fabric tore as I tumbled over the wall. For a moment, I thought I had twisted my ankle.

No, just a long rip in my pants. Bloodstains, too. Not that I was going to keep these pants much longer, anyway.

It was past eleven, and I wasn't sure how I was going to get into the main house, much less find Dolly's room, but I figured the first step in my as-yet-unformed plan was to find some clothes and blend in. Dropping trou and hitting the pool nude might have been clever when everyone else was wearing nothing, but I wasn't feeling as much an exhibitionist tonight. Besides, skinny-dipping at midnight was bound to raise eyebrows.

The employee parking lot was nearly empty. Lights were on down by the amphitheater, and I heard music playing. It didn't sound like a live band, and as I crept closely, I spotted a trio who were—

I stopped, and went back a few steps for a more unobstructed view.

I revised my theory about nocturnal naked time at the Hidden Palms Spiritual Center.

There were more groups of people roaming about near the amphitheater, and a few participants in the late-night bacchanalia were still wearing some of their undergarments, but they were definitely in the minority. It had been a long time since I had seen a free-for-all group grope like this—even longer since I had participated.

Everyone looked like they were having a good time—an important factor when you're getting it on out in the open air. I spotted Julia being held aloft by a pair of men, who were vigorously elated to be carting around a naked woman. One of the men stumbled, and she shrieked with laughter as all three of them turned into a pile of naked.

The wind shifted, blowing toward the house, and I caught the unmistakable smell of marijuana. Weed, boobs, and dicks. The holy trinity of late night bacchanalias everywhere.

I looked for other familiar faces, and I was sort of surprised to not see Gloria. Part of me figured she'd be party to this, if only for the casual familiarity of all the naked hoopla. I didn't see Dolly, but then I hadn't really expected to see her flashing across the lawn.

And the weight of everything came down on me, and I felt my knees wobble. Who was I here to save? And did they even need saving? Or was I the one who was running?

Shit, I had killed a man. In his own kitchen. With a fork.

Part of my brain started to rattle off the line numbers of the California Penal Code I had violated, and once it got started, it kept going. Manslaughter. Assault. Drug Trafficking. Impersonating a Federal Officer.

Watching the guests of the Hidden Palms Spiritual Center cavort and frolic in the bucolic buff, I was filled with an overwhelming sense of having lost something. I couldn't do what they were doing. That freedom—that innocence, if you will—was not a feeling I could ever have again.

What was I doing here? Was I trying to save myself?

My train of thought was interrupted by the unmistakable sound of a gun hammer moving into a cocked position. I started to turn and look over my shoulder, but a familiar voice told me to stop.

"Well, shit," I said. "I guess I'm having a bad day."

"You have no idea," said Deputy Franklin Hackman.

We skirted the amphitheater as we meandered away from the house. I wasn't in any rush to wander off into the woods and get shot, and Hack was the lingering voyeur-type. "Fucking perverts," he said at one point, which said something about the sort of lingering voyeur he was.

At one point, though, I could have sworn I saw Dolly. I slowed down, trying to look without being obvious, and Hack gave me a shove. "Keep walking," he snapped. I looked over my shoulder, ostensibly to give him the sort of bruised male ego glare he expected, but mostly to get one last look at the amphitheater from this angle before we passed it entirely.

There. Near the stage. Someone who wasn't as joyously caught up in all the nonsense. Talking to a tall, naked man with a full beard and a respectable package that was showing interest in the lady.

Was that Dolly?

Hack slapped my shoulder. "I'm not going to tell you again."

"You going to shoot me here?"

When he didn't answer, I kept walking. He had a destination in mind, and the late-night stroll was a chance for me to fit the remaining pieces into place.

"You're part of Team Weed, am I right?" I asked as we approached the back of the manicured grounds. The trees loomed, but there was a gap up ahead—a path leading into the woods. "You guys have T-shirts or something? Secret handshake? You get a bulk discount, right? For 'personal use.' That's what got David in trouble."

"Shut up, Bliss," Hack said.

"Where are they growing it?" I asked.

He wasn't answering my questions, but as I looked at the wall of trees ahead, I put a couple of things together. "They're growing it out there, aren't they? This place backs up to National Forest land. They've just wandered past the property line a little bit."

He shoved me harder, and I stumbled.

"Is that the game?" I asked. "If I guess right, you shove me around?"

"You're not DEA," he snapped.

"No shit," I said. "When did you figure that out?"

"You're fucking this all up."

"No, I'm pretty sure you and Potboy are doing that all on your own. I was just passing through."

"I don't believe you," he said.

"Okay, then," I said. "If I'm not DEA, and I'm not here by accident, then what I am doing? Who am I?"

He didn't like those questions any more than my other questions, especially because he didn't know the answers.

"Either I really am just an ex-con, ex-porn actor who is here by accident, or I have the most amazing cover story ever invented in the history of undercover police work," I said. "And if I'm not DEA, then what am I? AFT? Department of Justice? Part of some secret Cocaine Cabal who is trying to diversify into the weed business? Come on, Hack. Pick one or the other."

"He's looking for Gloria Griffin," a voice said.

Walking toward us from the house was Wilson and one of the Terror Twins. The sullen one. Wilson was wearing a long ceremonial robe with a hood, while the musclebound guy was wearing his white uniform. Balanced across his shoulder was a pole, and hanging from the end of the pole was an oil lamp, whose light was a flickering flame dancing at eye level. They looked like they were out trick-or-treating as Father, Son, and Holy Ghost.

"Who?" Hack asked.

"Also known as Gloryhole Gloria," Wilson continued. "Gloria Gusto. Glinda the Glorious Witch. Glory of the Whole—"

"Yeah, I've heard all of her nicknames, Wilson," I said.

"Is she the one . . . ?" Hack asked.

"She is," Wilson said.

"Well, damnit, Wilson. I told you we should have left them alone."

Wilson shrugged. "It's too late to be second-guessing our decisions now, isn't it, Deputy Hackman?"

"Them?" I asked. An unpleasant knot formed in my stomach.

"You'll find out soon enough," Wilson said.

"Where's the girl?" Hack asked.

"She's here," Wilson said.

"Where?" Hack asked, not willing to be put off so lightly.

"Terrance is bringing her."

"Is Terrance the one I punched in the dick?" I nodded at the guy holding the lamp. "And you're the one I kicked in the head, right?"

The flickering flame floated toward me, but stopped at a word from Wilson. "Ignore him, Sullivan. You'll get your chance soon."

"Is it going to be a fair fight?" I asked. "Or is Hack going to shoot me in the leg first?"

"I could just shoot you in the head right now," Hack said.

"Like you did Gloria?" I asked. That knot in my stomach was tightening, and I took a wild guess at cutting it in half with one stroke.

Hack raised his gun and walked up to me until the barrel pressed against my head. "You son of a bitch—" he started.

"Deputy," Wilson said. "Let's ease up on the drama, shall we?"

Hack fumed, and the barrel of the pistol dug into my forehead for a bit before he relented. But before I could move out of the way, he smashed me across the face with the gun.

I went down to my knees, and figured I'd let things settle in my mouth a bit before I said anything else.

"An interesting guess, Mr. Bliss," Wilson said. "But quite wrong."

I spat some blood out, and stood slowly, so as not to spook Hack.

"I shot Gloria," Wilson said. "And it wasn't in the head."

CHAPTER 25

I WOULD HAVE BEEN FINE DOING OUR WALK IN SILENCE, BUT WILSON had to talk. I really wanted him to shut up, because everything he said simply furthered the notion that the fundamental conclusion to this nature stroll was me getting a bullet in the head.

But that wasn't Wilson's style, apparently. So, yeah, still a mystery to solve.

I was getting tired of all these mysteries.

Gloria's downfall, as Wilson related it, was classic primetime drama, complete with the final tragic twist. A decade of drugs and hardcore films leached most of the beauty out of Gloria Gusto, and in a desperate struggle to remain the secret desire of young men everywhere, she had turned to plastic surgeons and cosmetic enhancements. They reshaped her into a marketable commodity, but the maintenance was expensive, and she had disappeared into a private world of pills and booze. She went in and out of rehab, finally ending up at Hidden Palms, where she had met Our Illustrious Founder and had been seduced by his religious fervor.

There were actual tenets to the First Church of the Holy Relic. Not that Wilson was a true believer. *El Illustro*'s message was—in Wilson's words—the "idiotic scripture of a narcissist shut-in who had watched *Sunset Strip* too many times as a kid." Immortality— as viewed by the First Church of the Holy Relic—was achieved by embracing your eternal close-up.

Yes, the "holy relic" the Church was predicated upon was nothing more than the body of the penitent acolyte, purified for perpetual preservation and relic-ification.

"Basically, when you die, the other members of this church are supposed to take pieces of you as relics?" I asked. "Like party gifts at the funeral."

"It was a metaphoric message," Wilson said.

"But Gloria took it literally."

"She did, and Elder Byron was attracted to her . . . devotion."

"*Devotion*, huh? Well, that's one way to put it," I said. "Did he know who she was?"

"He didn't care," Wilson said. "Her past as hardcore blow job queen only made her zeal more real. She desperately wanted to be transformed through a course of ritual cleansing and . . ."

"Dismemberment?" I offered.

Hack's frown deepened in the flickering light of the oil lamp. "They wouldn't have done it," he snapped.

Wilson gave him a look like you offer a child who thinks they're going to get their way when they throw a temper tantrum in the candy aisle at the grocery store.

The narrow path emerged from the forest into a wide clearing. In the center was a small stack of sticks that might have passed for a rain shelter once upon a time. Off to our right was a white pile of stones. Wilson indicated we should head for the white stones, and no longer confined to single file by the path through the woods, we spread out a bit as we headed across the clearing. Sullivan was on my left, between me and the leaning shack. When we got closer to the stones, I realized the circular shape was a well. A wooden plate sat on top.

"I watched some of her films," Wilson said. "That's why you seemed familiar. And then after your visit, I went and looked you up. You were in the lead in *Stroker's Lane*."

I hadn't thought about that film in a long time. "I may have been," I said.

"Wait? What?" Hack was feeling left out of the conversation.

"It was a movie," I said. "About a guy who worked in a bowling alley."

Sullivan reached the well, and he leaned the pole with the lamp against the ring of stones. He grabbed a heavy piece of rope attached to the wooden cover, and when he dragged it off the well, an entirely unpleasant smell rose out of the ground.

"That can't be good for potable water," I pointed out.

"It's been dry for a long time," Wilson said. "But it's deep."

"It had better be at the rate you're going," I said.

The smell coming out of the well suggested there were a couple of dead bodies down there, and if I had to guess, they were Gloria and *El Illustro*—two kids whose dreams had gotten away from them.

I caught sight of a light moving through the trees, and Hack whirled around at my reaction. Another lamp emerged from the woods, but this one was carried by hand. By Terrance, in fact. Who was alone.

"Where is the girl?" Wilson demanded when Terrance reached our little nocturnal party.

"Couldn't find her," Terrance grumbled. "She's not in the house, and if she's—"

"Cavorting with the other free-thinkers?" I supplied.

"Shut up," Hack snapped.

Terrance gave me a hard stare before he continued with his report. "If she's partying, then . . ." He trailed off with a shrug.

"Don't be such a prude," Wilson snapped. "I don't give a shit if they're fucking or sucking or whatever they're doing to each other in the woods. Go put your foot in some sphincters. Get them to tell you where the girl is."

"They're clients, Mr. Wilson. We shouldn't be . . ." Terrance was having some trouble with his directive, which was kinda sweet in its own way, but I still wasn't keen on his ultimate goal.

Wilson brought his right hand out of the deep pocket of his robe, and showed us the gun he had brought to this party. "Do what I tell you to do," he said. "Are we clear?"

"Yeah," Terrance said carefully. "I got it, boss." He gave me one last stare, and then started meandering back toward the main house.

"Now!" Wilson shouted after him, and after a second's hesitation, Terrance started to move a little quicker.

"It's hard to find good help these days," I said after the light from Terrance's lamp had vanished.

Wilson sighed loudly. "It's such a constant struggle," he said. He lowered the gun, but he didn't put it back in his pocket.

"So, this movie, this—what was it called?" Hack was clearly still hung up on my filmography.

"*Stroker's Lane*," I supplied.

"Yeah, *Stroker's Lane*. Was it . . . was it a pornographic film?"

"Yes, it was," I said. With a hint of pride in my voice. Hey, they say don't do the crime if you can't do the time. Own the things you've actually done, versus the things people think you've done.

"And you were in this piece of filth?" Hack asked.

"I was," I said. "It was my first starring role, in fact."

Hack looked back and forth between me and Wilson. "So, this whole ex-porn star thing. It's not a cover story? You really were one of those guys?"

"See what I mean?" Wilson said, looking at me. "Such a struggle."

He lifted his arm, and pulled the trigger on his gun.

There was a flash of light and a loud noise, and in the wake of all that, I heard Hack fall down. He groaned and coughed, and along with the fetid stench coming out of the ground, there was a tang of blood in the air.

"I think you missed," I said. "Maybe a little higher next time."

Wilson came closer, raising his pistol so it pointed directly at my face. "Like this?" he said.

"Yeah," I said. I swallowed a lump in my throat. "That should do it."

"Sullivan?" Wilson called. "Would you take Deputy Hackman's weapon away from him? And then . . . toss him in the well."

Sullivan came over to Hack, and there was a momentary scuffle, punctuated by a weak cry from Hack. I didn't want to take my eyes off Wilson. Hack was sobbing and pleading as Sullivan dragged him toward the well.

"Is the fall going to kill him?" I asked. "Or are we going to stand here and listen to him bitch and moan from the bottom for awhile?"

"*We?*" Wilson asked.

"I know, presumptive of me," I said. I nodded toward the well behind me. "Would it be easier if I threw myself in?"

"It would," Wilson said.

I thought about it for a second, and then shook my head. "I'm a terrible volunteer," I said.

"That's unfortunate," Wilson said.

"So, Gloria convinced Elder Byron that she was a perfect candiate for his church. Was that their plan? Letting her kill herself so *El Illustro* and the rest of his cult devotees could make necklaces out of her finger bones or something?"

Wilson laughed. "*El Illustro.* I like that."

I shrugged. "Well, you can keep it."

"I might."

I looked up at the night sky. "It got awkward for you, didn't it? If Gloria martyred herself that would bring all kinds of weird attention?"

"Certainly not the sort of attention we seek here at the Hidden Palms Spiritual Center," Wilson said.

"No, I suppose not." I sighed. "And Hackman? Where did he fit in this?"

"He brought in that kid—Boreal. Said the kid could help."

"But you were already distributing it, weren't you? It's not like you needed more help, right?"

Hack's voice became more strident, and I heard Sullivan smack him around until he shut up.

"Punching a man unconscious who is bleeding to death and about to be dropped down a well is cold," I said.

Wilson shrugged.

"I guess that's what happens when you're a bad shot," I said.

"I'm not a bad shot," Wilson snapped. His grip tightened on the gun, and the muzzle of the gun remained steady. Right at my face.

"Where did you shoot Gloria?" I asked. "Were you aiming for her face and missed?"

His gaze flickered to my chest. He frowned and lowered his aim.

He missed, I thought. *He doesn't keep the gun steady when he pulls the trigger.*

Something moved among the trees behind Wilson. It was impossible to tell what it was—but there was a definite flicker of light in the gloom.

I did a terrible job at hiding my interest.

Wilson smiled. "That's an old trick," he said. "And I'm not going to fall for it."

"Okay," I said. "But I had to try, right?"

The flicker solidified into a shape that was too small to be Terrance. My heart started pounding in my chest.

"Quite pathetic, actually," Wilson said. "Much like your acting."

"Hey, now," I said. "That's uncalled for."

He laughed. "What are you going to do about it?" he said. "Are you going to hit me?"

"No," I said. "But she is."

This time he looked, and Dolly hit him in the face with the stick she was carrying.

CHAPTER 26

As much as I wanted to stand and watch Wilson get smacked with a stick, I didn't need to be in line with his gun if he involuntarily pulled the trigger. Even if he was a bad shot. I darted to my left, and congratulated myself on the quick thinking as Wilson's gun went off. I took a half-second to be indecisive about helping Dolly or worrying about Sullivan, but when I heard Wilson cry out, my decision was made for me.

Sullivan, who had Hack halfway over the edge of the wall, dropped the wounded deputy when he realized I was coming for him. But instead of putting up his hands, he reached around to the back of his waistband. He had Hack's gun. I cut back the other way, trying to put the well between us, and when I saw the gun in Sullivan's hand, I dove for base of the well.

It wasn't big enough to play hide and go seek around for longer than a minute, and so I cast about for something that would improve my chances. Scrambling upright and putting my back to the stones, I shifted to the left and took a peek. Hack's face was right there, eyes open and staring. Blood, drooling from the corner of his mouth. I started and pulled back, just in time to hear Hack's gun go off. A divot of grass and dirt leaped into the air not far from the well.

If my head had stayed where it was, the bullet would have gone right through it.

I got off my ass and took a quick peek over the top of the well. Trying to spot Sullivan before he could Whack-a-Mole me with a bullet.

Also, corpses smell terrible. I didn't ever want to smell that stench again.

Sullivan had been on my right, close to Hack, and I crab-walked the other way, and almost got my ass shot off for going too slow. I scampered faster around the well, and then stopped abruptly. That's what Sullivan wanted, wasn't it? He wanted me to panic and go charging around the well. That's where he'd be waiting.

Or was he?

This was one of those stupid conundrums armchair theorists like to get all hot and bothered about. If this little rabbit went around the well to the left, and the hounds were waiting for him, then he was a stupid rabbit. But if he went back to the right, and the hounds were still figuring out which way to go, then he'd be running right into them. If he stayed where he was, the hounds were going to find him eventually.

This little rabbit was fucked, basically. Like I said, it was a stupid puzzle.

It doesn't matter, Mr. Chow used to tell me. *Because he is a rabbit, and they are hounds.*

So what's the rabbit supposed do? I had asked.

Stop being a rabbit, Mr. Chow had said.

I glanced at the pole leaning against the well. It was thicker than a normal broom handle and there was a metal cap at the top with a hook jutting from the cap. The storm lantern was made of heavy glass and metal, with a metal handle that was slung over the hook on the pole.

Rabbits were fast runners, but they couldn't win when cornered by a bunch of dogs with sharper teeth and nasty attitudes. They needed to change the game if they were going to win.

I didn't go for the pole. It was too unwieldy for the situation I was in. I went for the lantern instead.

My first try at grabbing the handle was nearly my last. Sullivan snapped off a shot, and the bullet blasted chips of stone out of the well. I pulled the pole over instead, and with my heart trying to leap out of my mouth and run away, I got my hands under the lantern before it hit the ground.

Gasping for breath, I unhooked the lantern from the pole, and scooted around the wall. Trying to change my position enough without giving it away. I stopped and listened for a second, and the only thing I heard was Dolly and Wilson wrestling. I couldn't tell who was winning, but there wasn't time to stop and figure out what was going on. I had to deal with Sullivan first.

I held the lantern by its handle. I couldn't do anything about the glow, which was—in hindsight—probably giving my location away as readily as if a spotlight were trained on me. And my night vision was a mess, so, really, what option did I have?

I stood up, looked for any target, and threw the lantern as soon as a shape registered in my brain.

Something punched me in the shoulder. It threw my aim off, but not by much. Unlike Wilson, I had decent hand-eye coordination. I had done all my own stunts in *Stroker's Lane*, after all. Including the bowling.

Sullivan tried to dodge the flying lantern, but his knees were still bothering him. The lantern hit him in the head, and bounced off. His head wasn't that hard, after all.

But the ground was.

The lantern shattered, and oil spattered everywhere. A second later, it all caught fire. Orange flames clawed up Sullivan's legs, and he squealed. He tried to get away from the fire, but all he managed to do was stumble through the film of burning oil, compounding his fire problem.

I went around the well, steering clear of the fiery ground, and I got close enough to Sullivan to hit him with the pole. "Drop and roll," I said, and I kept thumping him until the fire on his legs and chest was out.

Behind me, Hack made a noise. The fire had licked his shoes long enough to make his toes hot. He was trying to get away from the fire, but it surrounded him. He was trapped on the lip of the well.

"Crawl around," I shouted, indicating how he should retreat from the fire. I couldn't approach him directly, and even if I could, I wasn't overly fond of Deputy Hackman.

There was blood on his uniform and his face was twisted in pain. His boots were smoking, and a thin thread of fire was working its way up his right pant leg. Like a dog gnawing at his ankle.

I circled the well, and as I did, I looked for Dolly and Wilson. He was wearing a dark robe, and he could be lying face down ten feet away and I probably wouldn't see him, but Dolly had been wearing lighter colors. I should be able to spot her.

There was no sign of her. Just the old shack, leaning crookedly with its sagging mouth like a drunk who had been on a three-day bender.

Hack was canted at an angle, still shaking his leg like he could dislodge the flame. I leaned over. "Grab my hand," I shouted at him.

He looked over his shoulder, and his eyes were wide. He flailed for my hand, and we missed making contact. I grabbed his hand on the next pass, and I was about to warn him to be careful about leaning too far when there was a loud pop, followed by a series of smaller pops. Hack tumbled back, like he was trying to somersault over the mouth of the well. His hand was suddenly snatched out of mine as he fell into the well. His wail of fear and pain was cut short with a meaty thud.

I leaned against the well, and when I brushed a hand across my face, it came away bloody. It wasn't my blood. Was it Hack's? But how . . .

And then I realized what had happened.

Hack hadn't been trying to shake off an imaginary dog. He had an ankle holster, and he had been trying to get away from the gun strapped to his leg. The ammunition had cooked off, and it had done what it was supposed to do. Unfortunately his foot had been in the way.

Before I could more than shake my head at the universe's gruesome sense of humor, I heard a woman's scream.

My gaze snapped up to the old shack.

The front door. That sagging mouth.

It hadn't been open before . . .

CHAPTER 27

AT SOME POINT DURING MY FIRST CONVERSATION WITH NATALIE, she had told the story about *El Illustro*'s first year on this land—back when the world was new and dinosaurs still roamed the middle part of the continent. He had built a house for himself, and spent a year inside meditating or cogitating or masturbating—or whatever the coy term was for sitting in a shack by yourself for a year. Trying to see through your navel, or line up your chakras, or learn how to breathe through your pores. The sort of people who voluntarily remove themselves so as to "search for inner awakening" are full of it, frankly. They've never spent any time in real isolation. A week in solitary at CCI—hell, a weekend—was more than enough alone time for any human being.

Up here, in the woods, by yourself for a year? That's pure crazy. If you weren't when you started, you would be by the end.

The shack looked like it was an early project by a self-taught isolationist, and not in a good way. The walls leaned in, and the roof sagged along the front. There had been an attempt to build a porch, but the idea hadn't stuck around for more than a weekend. There were two windows in front, one on either side of the front door, and they were different sizes. The frame of the front door wasn't level, and as a result, the door hung crookedly.

It also made a lot of noise.

I backed up a step as soon as the door started its wretched groan. So much for sneaking up on whoever was inside. I crouched next to the uneven steps and waited for something to happen.

The door reached the end of its swing, and then started back. I waited until it was done. "Anyone home?" I called out.

I didn't get any immediate reply, but when I dared to peek inside the shack, a gun flashed. The bullet whizzed by my head.

"I take it that's a no," I said.

"Run away, Mr. Bliss," Wilson shouted. "I'll kill the girl if you come any closer."

"You're going to kill her anyway," I pointed out.

Wilson didn't bother to argue otherwise. We were at an impasse. I wasn't going anywhere, and there was only one way into the shack. Could I afford to wait him out?

The fire at the well was spreading to nearby grass. That was going to be another problem in a little while. I spotted a dancing light among the trees, like a lantern.

Like Terrance, coming back after hearing the gunshots.

Well, three problems now.

"Shit," I muttered, summarizing my feelings about this mess.

"You've made me realize something, Mr. Bliss," Wilson said, drawing my attention back to the shack.

"What's that?" I asked.

"I am going to kill her anyway, so—"

His sentence was punctuated by a gunshot.

You know what you learn in solitary confinement? You don't learn how to be a better person. You don't learn forgiveness. You don't invent a personal system of body building that uses your entire skeletal structure as a resistance machine against gravity. What you learn is patience. Every second that passes is one you will never get back, but you don't freak out and go all bug-fuck nutty about how much of your life is slipping by—second by second. You learn to how to wait. You learn if you've waited a year, then a week means nothing. If you've waited a month, then a day is like taking a long nap. And if you've waited a second, you want to wait one more. And one more after that. And one more after that.

And that's when I heard Wilson sigh.

I didn't hear the sound of a body falling to the floor. Or the last breath escaping from lungs suddenly slack. I heard nothing that sounded like it had come from Dolly. I just heard Wilson exhale.

And that's when I charged into the room.

There was another window on the wall opposite the front door, and given the location of the front door and how it opened inward, I expected that the original arrangement of the living area would be split in half. Living area on the right; sleeping and eating and what-not on the left.

If I was Wilson, I'd be on the left because that was where he'd get a second more to react.

I got three steps inside and ran into a black iron stove that was in the exact center of the room. I flailed my arms and knocked out the chimney pipe that went from the stove to a hole in the roof.

Wilson fired his gun, and the bullet whizzed by my head with an angry buzz. As I suspected, he was on my left. I dropped to the floor, hoping there was no other black furniture hiding in the murky and swampy darkness. He had been in the room longer than I, and his eyes had had more time to adjust. He would see me before I saw him.

There was a thick area rug under me. I crept forward several inches, and was starting to get a sense of the various shades of darkness, when I put my hand down on something soft and cool. Like a woman's leg, but one that had been lying out in the rain for most of the night. Not like the leg of a woman who was reclining, nude, on a bearskin rug in front of a roaring fire.

I jerked away, unwilling to face what a cold leg meant, and I backed into a fucking bell tree. Like one of those chains of mystical prayer bells hung on a thick cord near an altar. The ones you ring after you light a stick of incense and leave some paper money for the special godlings who watch over clumsy idiots or foolish women who insist on coming to the rescue of those same clumsy idiots.

I'm ringing your damn bells, little godlings. Are you laughing at me now?

I heard the distinct click of a hammer descending on a gun, and when nothing happened, I heard Wilson swear gently.

I exploded off the floor, and promptly tripped over Wilson, who was closer than I thought.

Wilson had been fussing with his gun, but he left off as soon as I got my hands on him. He tried to kick me, and I took a hit on the shoulder—the other one, thank you, little godlings in this crazy prophet's lean-to. I slipped under his leg and pushed it up. I was between his legs and I felt the fabric of his robe stretching beneath me. I banged around with my knees until I hit something soft, and he made a noise like a whoopee cushion.

The butt of his gun bounced off my head, and I tucked my chin down as I grabbed leg and robe. He tried to hit me again as I picked him up.

It's an old technique I learned from watching professional wrestling. Mr. Chow wouldn't have approved.

If you do it right, it's flashy and makes a lot of noise, but no one really gets hurt.

If you do it wrong, you will break something important in your opponent's neck.

I really hoped I was doing it wrong.

And I did it a couple of times to be sure.

The second or third time I heard the gun hit the floor.

Had Wilson shot Dolly? I hadn't been sure. If I had gone charging right in after he had fired his bullet in the dark, he would have put a bullet in me, fair and square. But I had waited, and he had sighed, and I thought maybe it had all been a ruse. That maybe he had just fired blindly into the wall of the shack.

But I wasn't sure, and so I kept banging him against the floor until he stopped squirming.

I dumped Wilson's body, and felt around for the gun. It had to be nearby. When I didn't find it right away, I wondered if it was under Wilson's body. I shoved it out of the way, and it was nothing more than a side of beef. Dead weight.

I spotted the gun finally. It had bounced farther away than I had thought.

And the reason I could see the gun was because Terrance was standing in the doorway of the shack, a lantern in his hand.

He looked at me. I looked at him. We both looked at the gun.

I got to it first.

CHAPTER 28

THE NIGHT CLERK AT THE HOTEL HAD HIS FEET UP ON THE DESK. His book had bored him into sleep, and his head was down. I banged on the glass, and he spooked. He nearly fell out of the chair, and disoriented about being caught sleeping on the job, he hit the button that unlocked the front door before he really processed what was going on. And once I was inside the hotel lobby and he got a better look at me, all the sleepiness fled from his eyes.

"Oh shit—" he started, and then he ducked to avoid getting hit by the coffee urn. It was mostly empty, and I was still running on adrenaline. I had picked the urn up and flung it without any concern for what or who I hit.

Oh, I had had lots of time to keep my anger stoked during the drive back from Hidden Palms. Lots of time to get more and more pissed off. Lots of time to fit all the pieces into the puzzle.

The coffee urn bounced off the counter, and took out the computer monitor on his desk. Stupidly, he popped his head up after a second, and I was right here. I grabbed his collar, hauled him up, hit him in the face a couple of times, and then hauled him over the counter and dumped him on the floor.

"Wha—wha—what do you want?" he blubbered.

I had Wilson's gun in my hand. There was one bullet left, chambered and ready.

"I'm checking out," I said.

"Oh, okay, okay. Just—you can just leave your key on the counter there," he said. The relief on his face was plain.

"But I'm not leaving quite yet."

"Oh." His face fell.

"The first night I stayed here. You remember that?" I shook the gun, and he nodded furiously. "I said I was looking for a few things.

175

Food. Drink. Drugs. Remember? And then I said I was going to get some girls, and that was when you got all nervous. I was just fucking with you then, but I'm not fucking with you now."

"Okay," he whined.

"You knew where I could get something to eat, didn't you?"

He nodded.

"And a drink, right?"

He nodded.

"And drugs."

I kicked him in the thigh when he didn't nod right away.

"Okay, okay," he shrieked. "I know where you get can some drugs."

I hauled him off the floor and threw him against the breakfast table. I grabbed one of the ceramic mugs and bounced it off his forehead.

"Ow!" he cried.

"Did you give those two bikers a key to my room?" I asked.

"Wha—ow!"

I picked up a third mug and asked the question again.

Holding his hands in front of his face, he nodded vigorously.

"Okay," I said. I stepped back from the table. "We're almost done."

He lowered his hands, saw the gun was still pointed at him, and then put them back up.

"Come on," I said. "I don't have all night."

His hands came down again.

"What's your name?" I peered at his shirt, trying to read his name tag, which—truth be told—had some blood on it.

"Mar—Marty."

"Okay, Marty, here's what we're going to do. We're going to go into the back room there, and you're going to make a phone call for me, and then we'll be done."

He started to whine, and I kicked at his foot. "Stop that," I snapped.

"You're going to kill me, aren't you?"

"Maybe," I said. "It depends on how long this all takes. You understand?"

He did, and he scrambled to be helpful. I followed him into the back office, and sat him down in the fancy chair behind the manager's desk. "Now," I said, making sure he could see the gun in my hand. "You're going to call Clint for me."

"Who?"

I smacked him in the forehead with the gun, and when he was done feeling the gash in his head and staring at the blood on his fingers, he nodded. "Okay, yeah, Clint. I know a guy named Clint."

"You're going to tell him you need to speak to him about citrus farming."

"About what?"

"Growing oranges, Marty. Clint is going to be real interested in what you have to say about splicing and stemming and all that shit they do to grow oranges."

Marty didn't believe me, but he was a good kid and did as I asked. It only took Clint ten minutes to get to the hotel. His bike rolled into the parking lot, and before the echo of its engine had faded, he was off the bike and through the front door of the hotel lobby, which I had left unlocked.

"What the hell is going—" He stopped in his tracks when he caught sight of me sitting behind the desk.

"Hiya, Clint," I said. And then I shot him.

He went down. I wiped down the butt of the gun and left it on the counter. I checked that the door to the back room was slightly ajar, and then I went into the lobby where Clint was thrashing about on the floor. The blood coming out of his thigh was making a mess on the carpet.

"Shit, Clint, that looks bad." I leaned against the breakfast table. "You should get that looked at."

He was shaking and sweating, but the look he gave me said if it weren't for the hole in his leg, we would be having a much different conversation.

Or trying to, at least. Last time, he had Brace do all the hard work, and look what happened to Brace?

"What the fuck are you doing?" he spat.

"Me?" I said. "I'm leaving town. I figured you and I should talk before I go."

"Talk? Talk about what?"

"About who's working for the DEA and who isn't."

That got his attention.

"Now, and you should correct me if I get any of this wrong, but there's a lot going on in Los Alamos, isn't there? We've got a bunch of guys farming weed up in the National Forest, and they're trucking it out through that hippy commune retreat center up there. And we've got a bunch of self-stylized crazy mother-fuckers who are running cocaine up and down the 101. It's not a bad stretch of road, really. You've got Lompoc and Vandenberg. No end of customers, right? And if you can get a guy in the sheriff's office who is happy to look the other way, well, then it gets really easy? Right?"

Clint didn't say anything, which I took to be tacit acknowledgment that I was telling a good story.

"Now, the DEA doesn't really want a gang of roughneck riders controlling the drug trade right next to a federal prison and an Air Force base, do they? That's bad for everyone, but they do like splashy announcements. If someone could just wrap this whole thing up in one nice package, they'd be thrilled. How am I doing so far?"

He had dragged himself over to one of the overstuffed chairs by the wall. He grabbed one of the pillows of the chair and applied it to the wound in his leg. He glared at me, and I smiled back.

"So, the DEA embeds a guy," I said. "They tat him up and give him some believable cover story—hell, maybe this guy has been doing the renegade biker dude cover for a couple of years now. Roaming from gang to gang, busting heads and pipelines as he goes. I mean, it's not as clever a cover as ex-porn star, ex-con, but it's functional, right?"

Clint spat on the floor. Some commentary, finally.

"So this guy is embedded for awhile, and he figures there's enough going on here for more than one guy to get a piece. There's not one crooked cop in the SBSO, there are two, which makes things a little more complicated, but not impossible. But then—and this is where it all goes a little sideways, right?—one of the cops gets nervous. He realizes if everything goes south, it's going to get hung on him. The other cop? He's not some patrol flunky. He's a rising star in the organization. He might even have aspirations for an elected position. It wouldn't be good for him to be involved in a drug scandal, right? Another reason for the first guy to get nervous."

I shifted my weight against the counter, not taking my eyes off Clint. Who was watching me as carefully as I was watching him.

"And so this guy—the patsy—he calls the DEA. He wants to cut a deal. Wants out. Wants protection. But not just for him. It turns out he's got some skin in this game—there are some innocents he wants protection for too. Now, the guy at the DEA who takes the call tells our boy they'll consider the deal. They call you, and you wave them off. You say it's not a good time. You don't have confidence that all the bad guys are going to get rolled up. You say to put the deal on hold.

"But the cop? He's persistent. He calls back. Really wants out. Even goes so far as to set up a passphrase to identify him to whoever they send out. Which, hell, you don't need because you already know who this guy is."

Clint grimaced as a wave of pain rolled through his body.

"But you're under a bit of pressure to deliver, aren't you? The office isn't happy this is still an open investigation. They might even be concerned that they've lost you. You've been doing this a long time. Maybe you turned on them, right? And so you're not sure they won't send a guy anyway. But, hey, if they do, you'll just intercept him and tell him to go home. Tell him that you have this covered. You'll tell him to be—what was it? Oh, yeah. To 'be smart.'"

He shook his head. "It's a bullshit story," he said. "Who are you going to tell it to?"

I shrugged. "Yeah, you're right. It probably is a bullshit story. But how about this one instead? Wilson, the guy who runs the Hidden Palms Spiritual Center? He's in charge of the pot farm, too. Not too long ago, Wilson killed two people. A man and a woman. They were threatening to bring too much attention to the whole area."

Clint sneered, clearly not interested in this story.

"No, really," I said. "Shot them both. Dumped their bodies in an old well on the property. Take a team up there and haul 'em out. Oh, and they'll find Deputy Hackman up there too. Right on top. That'll complicate things, won't it? Good thing he was shot by the same gun that shot the other two, right? Makes ballistics easy. And if you can find Wilson—maybe get swabs off his hands—you could prove he did all that shooting."

Clint licked his lips, and his eyes darted back and forth. He was thinking about my story.

I helped him along. "Okay, maybe it goes like this," I said. "Deputy Hackman gets nervous about all the drugs floating around the valley. Goes up to confront the man in charge. Gets popped and dumped for his trouble. But then something happens to Wilson, which makes it hard for him to deny any of this story, right? Maybe someone killed him in self-defense. Right after they got shot."

Clint narrowed his eyes, and his gaze hovered on my left shoulder, where the bullet from Sullivan's gun had gouged out a chunk of me. "Oh, this?" I pointed at the dried blood on my shirt. "Different gun."

I pointed at his leg. "The bullet in your leg? That came from Wilson's gun. The gun on the counter over there."

Clint looked, and I could see the wheels turning in his head. "It's not enough," he said finally. "There's still . . ."

"McCready and the rest of the CMFMC?" I nodded. "I know. What to do about them? If only you had someone who knew something about their distribution network who was willing to talk. Someone who realized everything was about to go to shit, and wanted to get on the right side of things before it was too late. Man, don't you wish you had someone like that?"

I pushed off from the table and came over to Clint. "You remember Marty?" I asked. "The kid who works the desk here. The one who called you and told you get your ass over here?"

Clint nodded slowly.

"He's in the back room. He's heard everything. He knows the gun is on the counter. He's probably wondering right now if he can get to it before you can. He's also wondering if I'm right. If he should be thinking about getting out before it all goes really, really south."

Clint stared at me, his breathing quick and shallow.

I put my foot on the pillow and pressed down. He screamed and writhed under me. I let him yell for a minute before I let off. Clint collapsed on his side, whimpering and moaning. There was more blood on the floor and on the pillow.

"That's for the three thousand dollars you took from me," I said.

And I walked out of the hotel.

I threw the saddlebags from Clint's bike onto the passenger seat of Dolly's car. It started on the first try, and I let the engine warm up for a second, idly watching the lobby. Clint was crawling toward the counter, but it was taking him a long time. Eventually, he'd get to the gun.

Which was empty. The last bullet was in his leg.

I doubted Marty knew the first thing about firing guns anyway.

I slipped off the handbrake and drove out of the parking lot, heading north. Going to find the 101.

In the backseat, the blanket moved. Cautiously, a head poked up. "Is it over?" Dolly asked.

I glanced up in the rearview mirror and smiled at her pale face. There was dried blood in her hair. Wilson had actually tried to shoot her in the shack, but he had missed.

"Yeah," I said. "It's over."

"Where are we going?" she asked.

I glanced at the saddlebags on the seat next to me. I could smell the faint odor of men's cologne and dog urine. "North," I said. "I thought maybe we'd find a place with sandy beaches and decent waves."

"Are we going to get naked there?" she asked.

The lesson Our Illustrious Leader of the First Church of the Holy Relic had learned during his year of solitary contemplation was that it was easy to be alone. Gloria had learned that lesson too, during all those years of working in the adult film industry. And they both thought that finding someone who understood that isolation and who wanted to save you from it was nigh impossible.

I looked at Dolly again in the mirror, and thought about surfing and lying in the sand.

"Every day," I said. "Just you and me. Every day."

I liked to think that maybe they were wrong about that, in the end.

ABOUT THE AUTHOR

Harry Bryant lives in the Pacific Northwest with a house full of pretty books.

Butch Bliss will return.

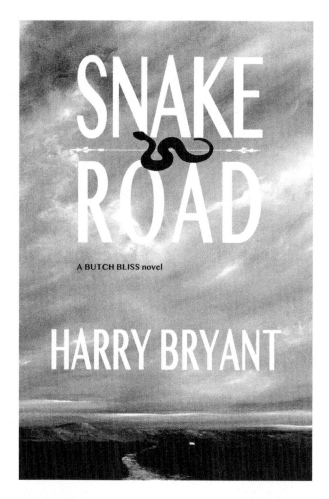

SNAKE ROAD

A BUTCH BLISS novel

HARRY BRYANT

ISBN: 9781630231033

CPSIA information can be obtained
at www.ICGtesting.com
Printed in the USA
LVOW03s0244120517
534225LV00005B/6/P